GW00750616

SUN
FLOWER

Published by The Blue Print Works Ltd.

Paperback ISBN-13: 978-1-7397633-5-0
eBook ISBN-13: 978-1-7397633-6-7

Printed in the United Kingdom

Cover design by Ryan Slaven

Layout by www.spiffingcovers.com

Find out more here: www.aleksandrjarid.com

SUN FLOWER

Aleksandr Jarid

"Why are all lessons in life taught to us in every minute of our existence, yet we only learn in the last moments of reflection?"

Aleksandr Jarid 2022

Was difficult to write this narrative novel at a time when one was facing the darkness with little or no light to guide. But darkness can only last if there is light for contrast. Eventually the light starts to shine again.

The winter months of 2021 when most focused-on Christmas and new year, others felt the loneliness and emptiness. But with time, processing and becoming a better version, creativity and fulfilment starts to endure through.

Thank you to The National Gallery in London for putting up with my obsessive visits to study the paintings. Special mention to the security guard Emilio in room 41. Your kindness and infectious smile are a reminder to always look on the bright side.

Thanks to everyone at Pasta Brown in Covent Garden for feeding me while I plotted and planned.

The long evenings and nights on Sundays and Mondays at Lyaness bar. You guys made the creative process so fun and kept me focused to get this book done. Many more evenings like that please!

The usual suspects : Charlie (drinks and late-night chats); Anisah (walks and talks); Ryan (creative visuals); Paige (boss); Beverley (lifeline); Eva (the ice cream); Chloe (from a distance but so close); Simba (useless in the most useful manner); Gabriel (will miss your dedication). You all rock!

PROLOGUE

"Get over it, Hugo, and do something useful with your time and life. Like, sort your finances out. Get a proper job. Get your relationship back on track." Those words are all I heard from everyone who I tried to explain my work to. They all listened, well, seemed to listen, but it was evident that they all couldn't care less for my research. No, I am not obsessed with my work. It's my passion and it's a passion that will one day lead to a great discovery. Then they will all look at each other and say, "You know what? Hugo was right after all. We should have listened to him." But by that time, it will be too late for them all to pick up the phone and congratulate me, as I would have more important things to take up my time.

I know it is out there. The Americans did not destroy it in the bombing of Japan during the Second World War. I just need the opportunity to find it and prove that the masterpiece of Vincent van Gogh survived. Once I do that, my finances will sort themselves out. My relationship aspects will fall back into place. She will see that. And all the doubters that have crossed my path will be eating their own words.

I can't fucking wait.

1

Now

I suppose it was inevitable that the path was going to be turbulent. My eyes close, seeing the images flash through my mind as clear as a summer's day, creating a kaleidoscope of torment right there in front of me. The words tragic, beautiful, trauma, demons, destiny, peace, calm and chaos all come to mind. All those words string together to create a sad, beautiful love affair that I have had with life. I am not sure what I am now more afraid of. To keep my eyes closed or to open them and take in my surroundings. To take in the now and here and what is to come. At least if I stay with my eyes shut off from the world, it will keep me insulated in the false blanket I have around me.

But that is a choice that was taken away from me at birth. This is the inevitability of all this. Not that I believe in fate being written down and all that bullshit. But, from birth, the cascade of events are put in place out of our control. Then, bang! Suddenly, when we are aware of the ability to make choices or decisions, we really do not have that true honest ability if the first few years, as a child, we had that mutual respect for kindness and empathy ripped away from us. *"Fuck it. Shit happens. Deal with it."* Easy words for someone to say, but the reality is that no one will truly ever understand the agonising plague that festered deep within.

Abandonment issues and co-dependency is what my therapist termed them. Well, that was much better than the narcissistic label I was terrified of having. I recall the day when I panicked after reading endless papers and articles on the Internet for traits of narcissistic behaviour and, obviously, I could attach myself to every one of them. Including the published paper that suggested there was a link with eyebrow shape. Of course, I rushed to the mirror to scrutinise my eyebrows and, low and behold, I diagnosed myself as a fully-fledged narcissist. When I took my learned findings to my next therapy session to discuss, the exact words from Fiona, my therapist, was, *"Hugo. You are not a narcissist by classification."*

I sat unconvinced. Shaking like a leaf and anxious inside that I was forever programmed to be full of chaos. She asked me how I was feeling right then when I thought I was a self-diagnosed narc. *"I am shitting it that I am a horrible person and my behaviour explains everything that I have become and that I will not ever change and keep–"* She cut me off by raising her hand and calmly saying, *"Narcs do not have these feelings if they are truly a narcissist. You have several other traumas that have caused clear abandonment issues and co-dependency. But you are not a narcissist."*

I sat there, trying to take it in that I was not forever damaged and that there was hope. But when the mind latches onto something, it is always difficult to remove it from the front seat. Even worse, is burying it in the boot of the car for it to rear its ugly, destructive head later on.

"Hugo. You done in there?"

My thoughts are brought back to today with a knock at

the door and the voice of Femi. He has such a thick accent from his village, around 50 miles west of Bulawayo, the second largest city in Zimbabwe.

"Be out in a few minutes," I answer.

I wish I could leave the light out and end it all now, for me. How many times in the past have I tried to do that? But, it always just stayed as a dark thought in my mind. I was never brave enough to follow through with anything. Well, brave or selfish? Not sure what lens would be better to view suicidal ideation from. But the thoughts and the darkness manifested and travelled along happily in the background, deep in the cortex of my mind. To emerge at regular intervals to remind me that I was fucked and would never be 'normal' or 'happy' or 'content'. Words that feel alien to me. Even the tone of those words sound so soft and pathetic to me.

"Well, get a move on." Femi's strong, confident voice again from the other side of the door. "We can't stay here any longer. It's not safe."

I sigh heavily. I am well aware that any of my best days have long been left behind, that is if I had any in the first place. There were a few perhaps contented times. But now, I am sure that I will need to run with my eyes closed, as the rest of my days, on reflection, will never contain any of my previous best days.

I take in my surroundings again. Looking around this sparse room that oozes nothing but neglect. The heat wafts in from the small window, high up on the wall to my left. The glass broken from the window frame and metal bars stand across the opening to create a feeling of safety. The heat is punishing in here. I have no idea how Femi deals with it so easily. He always seems so calm with no sweat on his smooth, tight skin. Fucking genetics. Whereas I have had constant damp patches all over me ever since we hid out here. My forehead has been a constant pool of dripping, salty sweat that travels down my face. My neck uncomfortable with the heat rash and irritated of the dampness.

Standing up, I peel my shirt off. The sink is covered in dust and remnants of brickwork and plaster from the walls and ceiling above. Struggling with the tap, as it is so stiff, I notice how weathered my fingers seem now. Managing to finally turn it, I feel the water on my face, which should have relieved me. But it only reinforces the shit situation I find myself.

"Finally. You ready?" I walk out of the bathroom to find Femi checking the contents of his travel bags. He looks over at me when I don't answer. "Look, Hugo. Don't worry. This is how it will be for a few more days, but we need to keep on the move. You good?"

"Y-y-e... yeh, it's fine." Fuck, I am stuttering. "The heat is just getting to me." I can hear my own voice, tired, defeated and anxious, all encapsulated in an air of hope that Femi has a plan. I must trust him. I *need* to trust him. He better not fuck me over.

"Good, now get your gear together. We will use the midday heat to get to the riverbank. We have a boat waiting for us there. Those German pricks won't hunt us in the sun. Their skin can't take it."

The room is a mess. I slept on the floor while Femi had the bed. We only had perhaps two hours to rest and recharge. As Femi said, it's not safe here now. This disused shack will soon draw attention to others if we stay here to use as refuge a while longer. My backpack has become lighter as the days have been going. Using up supplies. It was too risky to travel using the main routes such as public transport or roads to drive. We had no choice but to use the cover of the terrain from Luxor to the meeting point along the river, to get us safe passage to Cairo by boat.

As I pack the dry clothes that were washed a few hours ago into the bag, I take note of the time. 11.26 AM. How the hell can it be well over 30 degrees Celsius already?

"Who is your contact again to get us to Cairo?" My voice has a waver of uncertainty in it.

"Dude. Can you just calm down and understand that I have this? It's my cousin who has worked on the same shipping containers for the last 15 years. We can trust him."

I can hear my own thoughts reminding me, *"Do not push him away and sabotage, as always. Allow the trust."*

"I know. I know. I'm sorry, Femi, but this isn't something like a sightseeing trip we are going on. Does he know what we carry?"

"No. I have not told him, or indeed anyone. He may be family, but we do not want to have anyone else put at risk with this. Last thing we need is them threatening others to get to us. To get to *it.*"

I like how Femi calls the object 'it'. I feel a tap on my shoulder. The heavy hand of Femi.

"We have done well, Hugo." His voice now softer than earlier. He can sense my need for reassurance. All those years of therapy and I still need reassurance. I am thankful for his understanding. "But right now we need to get the fuck going." I am also thankful for his direct tone.

Finishing the packing and zipping up my bag, I sit on the edge of the bed, its mattress no more than a thin, bare piece of foam that has lost all aspects of padding or recoil properties. My army grade boots are still going strong. They contain torturous heat insulating properties not needed in this weather, but at least they are lasting. Finishing lacing up my right boot, I look over to the chair in the corner of the room. That corner, in the shade, has the enticing pull of comfort and calmness to it. It would have been the best spot to take refuge from the heat surrounding us. But in that corner, resting on the chair, something commanded the right to have that spot. Something that sat tall on the cushion, comfortable and confident in the chair. Femi and I being the guardians of it. As I stare at *it*, it scares the crap out of me. This 98cm by 69cm object, tightly encased and insulated to withstand all manner of external atmospheric insults. Yet, there is probably no manner of protection that would keep it from the greed and selfish aspects of humans that would hunt for it. Humans that would lie, cheat and kill for it.

The zip closing on Femi's bag gets my attention. He looks over at me with his dark eyes. He knows exactly what I am thinking. Where my thoughts are. We both look towards the chair. Femi moves slowly towards the chair and reaches carefully to grab the rectangular object by its sides and brings it over to the bed where I sit. I stand to make room and, before he lays it down, I smooth out the sheets on the mattress as best as I can.

"Check the top seam," Femi directs me. It's the same routine we have. Every time we set off. The same checks. I move to the edge of the bed to see the top of this rectangular casing. Carefully, using my eyes to visualise any breach of the seam. The corners need particular attention as they fall to the longer side of the object. Femi stands back a few feet away from the bed. He needs me to concentrate.

"Visual seems intact." My voice low. I can feel my heart pounding and the sweat that I thought was washed off in the bathroom, now covering my face and neck.

"Good. Proceed to tactile check."

As I step closer to the edge of the bed, I wipe my sweaty palms on the side of my cargo pants. Leaning over the bed, I feel a drop of sweat down the side of my temple, making its way to my cheek, ready to fall onto the bed. I make sure it does this before I am close to the object for inspection. Although I know my fingers will not actually touch the object resting within, I cannot help but feel its presence penetrating like an electric shock into my fingers, coursing through my entire body.

"Hugo…"

The prompt from Femi reminds me that I need to stay focused. My fingers, slowly and methodically, run the course of the intricate seams along the edge, from one corner to the other.

"Tactile inspection intact and complete for the top edge." I regain my composure with that statement and realise that I have been holding my breath all this time.

Femi steps forward to my side. I make room for him by walking over to the opposite end of the bed.

"Visual check of lateral edge intact. Proceeding to tactile inspection." Femi is much stronger and focused in his conviction. His large, spade-like hands with fingers like dense wooden beams make the longer edge easy work. He takes longer at the two corners with increased concentration. "Tactile inspection complete of lateral edge and intact."

I glance at my wristwatch. 11.42 AM. I step towards

the foot of the bed and am ready for my duty to inspect the lower margin. This time with more confidence and vigour.

"Visual check intact." It takes me less time to move to the tactile check than the previous. "Tactile check complete and intact."

I can sense Femi's sigh of approval because I was more conscious of time with the section check. He responds with the same effort of efficiency once he completes his final long edge checks.

We both stand at the foot of the bed looking at what lies on the mattress. We both know that no words are needed or are comprehensive enough to explain the magnitude of what rests there.

"Get the harness." I walk over to the dirt-filled, ripped curtain that is drawn over. On the floor is the tangled harness that we attach to carry this object, safely and securely, on our backs, like it is our own child.

"I will take the first carry." I gather the confidence to offer before Femi takes the lead. We both ensure the harness is correctly and securely attached to the casing. I stand in the middle of the room with my back facing the bed and looking away from Femi. I can just make out the faint outline of what seems to be a lizard clinging to the wall in front of me. I use this as my focus point. I can hear Femi's slow breath as he walks forward and picks the casing up. I feel the flat of it against my back. I am too scared to move any muscle in case it disturbs this need for concentration. The straps of the harness fall over my shoulders while there are two swinging down beside my legs.

"Ready for you to secure." Femi's voice behind me as he holds the case in place on my back. On his instruction,

I take the shoulder straps and buckle them tightly to the corresponding buckles beside my legs. I pull them tight and let Femi know. He then passes another buckle around my waist and I secure it across my torso.

The heat is unbearable standing here so still. There is no breeze and my clothes are soaked through with sweat. Femi comes to stand in front of me, obscuring the view of my new lizard friend, cool as a cucumber, not anything out of place. He pulls at each buckle and harness and tightens the right shoulder's buckle slightly. He stands back to admire his work.

"Ready?"

"Are we ever ready?" And with my reply, Femi picks up our bags, one in each hand, and moves to the door. He opens it slightly; the rays of sun force themselves in, rushing to illuminate the floor. I see the dust fairies dance around in the beams.

"Let's go."

2

Before

"Fuck, fuck, fuck!" How can I turn my thoughts off? Walking around the streets I thought I would be less anxious than this. I felt suffocated indoors, alone, flicking through the television and browsing the music on Spotify simultaneously, so I decided I needed to feel safe outside, around others. But bloody hell! London in December with stupid Black Friday sales with nothing but couples, families, friends and colleagues. All talking and laughing and having 'normal' interaction. I can't process this at all. Coming out of Bond Street's tube, I hit the sea of bodies, weaving along the pavement. Yeh, sure, I look in control on the surface. Pleasant, confident and at one with myself. But, I am the master chameleon. Take away all the colours and what is left is something that I have struggled with since as far back as I can remember.

I spot the bright lights of the Christmas decorations overhead, illusions of falling stars. Blue lights flashing lazily against the dark evening sky above. They remind me of *The Starry Night* by van Gogh. Damn, that is also why I came out. I have some research work to do. Whatever I need to do to get out of this mood, I need to, as I have to concentrate on work.

"Sorry, mate. Didn't see you there." A boulder-like man of short, round, solid build rushes past me, knocking into my side. Before I have a chance to say it's OK, he is out of sight amongst everyone else surrounding me. They all seem to have a purpose in their chaos. Compared to just the disorganised chaos in my mind. I feel totally unsettled and overwhelmed. It's not a panic attack. I have never actually had a panic attack in the past. I get anxious, yes, but I deal with that emotion by projecting confidence and becoming defensive and, damn right, a monster to those closest. Hence, I have no one close left to me. I am the master at burning those bridges and just manipulate and push people away to reinforce my abandonment behaviour. Sounds like I have insight into what I do, so why the fuck can't I recognise it at the time and stop it?

I can see a safe spot in the window across the street in that coffee shop. Perhaps, paradoxically, caffeine will help calm me down. I never sleep anyway, so bollocks to the caffeine hit. I may as well have my IBS play up.

"Just a flat white, please." I ignore the tempting cakes displayed on the counter under the glare of the lights.

"Sure, just have a seat and I will bring it over."

I grab the seat by the window. Right. Need to get on top of what has sparked this episode of how crap I am feeling, as I will get no work done at all this evening. Already the dread and doom at the thought of trying to fall asleep later, in bed alone, is fucking with my head.

"Here you go." My flat white arrives. I look up at the attendant, spaced out, thinking, *"Where am I?"* I get a gentle smile back and am left to my thoughts again.

I need to stop doing this. I want to look through my

phone, get onto the good old Google pages and research everything about 'fear of abandonment' and 'co-dependency'. I have lost count of how many times I have done this. I doubt anything new will appear on the first few pages of the search that I have not already read. I keep wishing to believe that I will be my old self again, but then the bloody reality hits and I remember that I have never been a normal 'old self'. Ever.

I scroll through my contacts list and find the number for my therapist. I am sure she is getting sick and tired of me now. Is it two years now or three? I can't remember. I blank it out because, 1) with the cost of all the sessions over those years, I am sure I could have afforded a mortgage; 2) all those sessions and I'm still fucked up. But, that is the only safe place I feel I have of late.

> 'Fiona. Thank you for holding my hand through this. I know it's your job, but I also want to say thank you, as it's the first time in my life I am facing everything I locked away and I feel safe doing this with you. And if it means I need to do this for life to have a life then I want that journey. Thank you again. Best, Hugo.'

I hit the 'send' button. Not sure what I was hoping for with this message. Probably my typical need of trust and constant reassurance to be given, for validation. But will I also push this trust away? Because that is what I have been through ever since I can remember, as a child. I feel so shaky and fragile inside. My legs ache sitting here. I need to move them under the table, like they are thin pieces of glass and will shatter any moment. This is what happens when I always run on cortisol and adrenaline due to lack of sleep and of never being able to switch off.

I stare at the message I have just sent, sipping the flat white, keeping the screen lit on the phone. What was I thinking? I know she will not respond. She is a professional and knows how to keep boundaries. Here I go again... not understanding boundaries. Pushing them. Feeling rejected and abandoned again by someone whom I trust. It's been at least two minutes and still no reply. Fuck it! She is just like everyone else. Letting me down. Why did I ever think it was going to be anything different? Bitch.

No, no, no. Calm down. I know this is coming from that dark place again. It is irrational and I am processing this all wrong.

Damn, my flat white is finished. I look around me. Take in the surroundings for the first time of coming in here. It's actually quite cosy. Surprisingly not as busy as I thought, what with all the crowds outside. I suppose everyone is all caught up in the savings they can make before Christmas. That is another aspect that I need to really work on. I always feel I need to 'buy' people's affection and friendship. I am programmed to think that people will only want to know me if I can please them and that invariably always ends up with me overspending and overcompensating. Insecurity screams out. Rushing to be attached way too soon in relationships and then pushing those same people away and using control to do that and then blaming them for letting me down again and abandoning me. Arghh, my mind is spinning. Coming out of the apartment was supposed to make me feel better, not worse.

My phone lights up. A message. Jump on it. Quick!

'Hello Hugo.
I'm glad it feels safe enough to do… not an
easy thing. And yes, it does need to be walked
through carefully and gently, so that you can
live life to the full from here onwards. You're
doing well. Keep going. You have good friends
to support you and you will come through all
this.
Take the best of care, have a good weekend and
see you next week.
Fiona'

I smile. She made an effort to message back. She *does* care. Of course she does. She is a professional. She obviously knows I am in that horrible spiral at present where everything seems so overwhelming. At least I feel someone listens and will understand the meaning behind my potential toxic behaviours. I hate the person I become at times.

"Would you like anything else, sir?" The attendant standing by the table reaches for the empty cup.

"No, no. Thank you so much. Just the bill, please."

That message from Fiona has given me the needed kick up the butt to get on with things and focus.

The cold snap catches me as I step back out onto the street. I am allowed to put my phone away for a while. I have attached my phone as my security to self-validation, hoping people will reach out to me, but I need to understand that I do not need to have others validate me. What was that saying Charlie told me once? The Latin meaning of intimacy comes from the word *intimare*, which means 'bring into' and that comes from *intimus*, which means 'innermost'. Need to keep reminding myself of that. I need to look into myself to validate myself. Not to others to do that for me. Easier fucking said than done.

Need to put my gloves on, anyway. Can't check the phone with my gloves on, so that's another good form of contraception with my neediness. At least I remember my purpose of coming out now. To get to the bookstore before it closes. Hopefully, they will have the book I need in stock. I suppose I could always order it online, but I find bookstores a place of romantic safety. Romantic in the sense of being surrounded by so many stories, so many inner thoughts, so much hope, so much tragedy, so much pain and suffering and so much laughter and happiness. All the emotions that I need to have balance with. I let the books surround me with those aspects and hope that those emotions will seep into me and mould me with some magic form of osmosis. But, alas! It does not work that way. In fact, it just reinforces that I am devoid of such attachment and the destructive behaviours are ingrained into me. Part of my DNA. Fuck, I am doing it again. Just get to the bookstore and see it as nothing more than that.

3

Now

The heat was so unforgiving. Femi made the terrain seem so effortless with his long strides. Every now and then, looking back at me to ensure I was close behind, carrying our precious cargo. Sweat poured off my face as I looked down at the uncertain stability of the ground below me – a mixture of sand, bush, tree stumps and mud. We had to stay as close to the riverbanks as possible, using the foliage of the dense trees and bushes as cover. We needed to weave off the bank and deeper inland into the bushes every now and then. I trusted Femi's compass to get us to our intended pick-up point. According to Femi, it was about a three-hour walk, give or take, to the pick up point just north of Luxor. The boat would then take us safely to Cairo. I pray.

"Hey," I panted. He does not hear me. "Femi!" a little louder.

Damn, just how does he manage to look so strong and calm?

"What is it, Hugo?"

"Let's have a break, please. My back and this heat are killing me. This fucking heat!"

I can tell Femi is disappointed and agitated at my pathetic endurance effort. But what the hell did he expect from a city boy? Give me an Uber any day.

He pulls out his military-issue watch from under his sleeve and does something that looks like more than just checking the time. I feel embarrassed at my cheap imitation of that watch that I ordered from Amazon a few days before I left London.

"We can have ten mins max, OK?"

I feel relieved at the understanding from Femi to give me a break.

"Thanks, man. I just need to get my hydration back and let my legs rest a bit."

I am well aware that I will not be able to take the cargo off my back, even in the rest period, as the risk of anyone following us and us needing to get going, is too great. Femi puts the bags down by a bush that seems to have some red berries falling from it. He takes out a couple of the two-litre bottles from one of the backpacks, rearranges the other contents in the bag, zips it up and flattens the surface.

"Here, come and sit on this bag. It will let you keep your back straight so the weight will ease as you rest."

No wonder he comes with a high price and recommendation. He knows his stuff. More than anything I want to kick my boots off, release the burden of this package from my back, lay flat on the ground in the shade and pour the litre of water all over me. But I settle for sitting on the bag and sipping from the bottle slowly and allowing each drop to coat the vast, rugged, dry nature of my mouth and lips.

"How much further do you think we are?" I ask Femi, who has not yet sat down. He is pacing around, looking back in the direction we just came from. In surveillance mode, as always. He looks back at me sitting and slumps onto the floor, on the spot. I pass him the bottle of water and he takes it with one big, strong, confident grip. I notice the comparison of our hands as they momentarily hold the same bottle – my olive skin, with nail cuticles that are peeling and the reddening rash of heat. I can see how there is slight muscle wastage on the back of my hand, with the tendons of my fingers straining.

"We have probably another two hours' worth of journey. We have made good time so far." He gulps the water. I can see his strong neck muscles stabilise as he swallows. "You doing OK?"

"Yeh," I answer, looking away deep into the wilderness that surrounds us.

"Hugo."

I hate when I am put under the spotlight like this. Always feeling like I am wearing a sign around my neck saying, *'Fragile. Handle with care'*.

"I am OK, man. The journey has kept my mind focused on just how bloody unfit I am. All those fucking gym memberships for nothing." I give a nervous chuckle, which Femi sees straight through, keeping his steely gaze on me. I sigh. "I am OK. Honestly. And thank you for understanding and checking in. But I am good."

"Good. Because all I am interested in is what you are carrying on your back," Femi smiles as he responds sarcastically.

I find the gentle sounds that surround us calming in the heat. There is the rustle of leaves and various songs from birds that no doubt Femi would be able to name, one by one. The sound of the shoreline coasting along as our companion on this journey. It reminds me of the evenings I would sit on my balcony, back in London, listening to the waves along the pebble shore as the boats went past. On occasions, the peace disturbed by those nonsense party boats. But here, in total contrast, is just the total peace of nature and harmony that puts me at some aspect of inner peace. Fuck, fuck, fuck! I just acknowledged that I feel at peace. This is seen as a positive emotion, which will automatically make me want to self-harm in taking it away and being made to feel bad and guilty for feeling that positive emotion in the first instance. I cannot afford to have a freak-out now.

"Shall we get moving?" I shift on my makeshift seat with urgency. I need to focus my energy and thoughts on something else that will drain the negative thoughts from coming into my frontal cortex.

Femi narrows his eyes and I can see the sun breaking through the shade of the trees and falling on his face, making him seem even more spiritual than he already is. He glances at his super fancy watch again. "We have another few mins if you need."

"No, I am–" Femi interrupts with urgency by putting his hand up and fingers across his lips. He indicates by pulling on his right ear that he heard something of concern. He gets down on all fours and crawls over to me.

"Stay here." These were the only words that Femi said looking directly at me. And then he crawled away, into the thick bush, and all I saw were the branches moving back into place, covering his movements.

I feel more alert all of a sudden. The draining thoughts I had a few moments ago are suppressed now as I have this trauma and hypervigilance to replace it. I can feel my chest aching with adrenaline. I know I will find it difficult to run at great speed with the package on my back, but I will have to muster the technique to do so if it comes to it. In a moment, I become aware of the silence. The birds have stopped singing their tunes. Fuck! I have seen enough films to know that this means they have been spooked into silence. I look and focus my eyes at the exact spot that Femi disappeared to, in the bush. Sweat drips into my eye. The salty nature stings my cornea making me blink and my vision blurs. I check the buckles of the harness, ensuring they are tight and in place, ready for me to stride as soon as I need to. Why the fuck are the birds not singing? My hand clears all the dampness from my face. It's dripping off me like a tap now, not just the heat but also the nature of this situation. Come on, Femi, where are you?

I can see my chest moving up and down, enhanced by Femi's disappearing act. My breathing is probably at a rate of 40 breaths a minute. I turn to look at the direction of the shoreline, the direction that I need to start moving if I do not get a sign that Femi is returning. But how the fuck will I know where I am going? Sure, I can keep following the river, but it has so many streams and paths, I will have no clue. Fuck. Now I wish I had paid more attention to Femi and the location of where we're headed.

Suddenly, I feel a hand cover my mouth from behind. Tight and strong. I can smell what seems to be wet soil on the fingers. The fingers tighten around my lips. I can feel the thumb along my jaw. The breath of this person, warm and forceful next to my right ear. Fuck! This is it. I make a fist with my right hand; ready to resist whatever is in store for me.

"We have to move. Now."

The voice of Femi in my ear. For fuck's sake.

4

Before

The weather has turned to create more of an icy cold snap today. London has the winter sun to it this afternoon. From inside, looking out, I could be fooled into believing that it is warm if I were to ignore everyone wearing thick overcoats and gloves. Been sat here at the dining table all morning, going through the book that I got last night, *The Turbulence of van Gogh*. What a crap effort at being original for a title of a book. Like that title adds anything to what the world does not already know about the great artist.

I am trying to ignore the pile of letters that have made their home on the far edge of the table by keeping my eyes from them. The white and brown window envelopes, resting haphazardly, unopened. The more I try not to notice the letters and pretend they are magazines or just junk mail, the more my eyes are drawn to them. I know they will be invoices that need paying. Bills that I have put off for a while. Fines. As long as there are no court summonses hidden amongst them, the rest can wait. Fuck it. The court summonses can wait also.

I can't focus on this book. I am not sure what else I can learn from printed literature on van Gogh anymore. There is not anything new that jumps out at me. Coffee may help me focus. As I open it, the fridge reinforces the nature of my emptiness. Nature being with the fridge contents and the general nature of my life. Three eggs left in the carton and a half-full carton of oat milk. Oh, what a bonus; I also spot a jar of Mexican salsa in the fridge door. Party time for me. Whoop, whoop! Extra strong coffee to focus on the day.

It always gives me comfort and that slight air of excitement when I make myself a coffee at home. Simple pleasures and triumphs. I have to take them when I can. Those are the small positive steps forward for me. That's what Fiona, my therapist, would say. Small, baby, positive steps. A major leap would be actually learning to cook at home. Well, shop and then cook. The fucking issue is that when shopping it's always so evident that I am shopping for one, eating for one, living for one. That, in its manner, reinforces that I am alone and then bang! Self-pity, insecurity, my need for co-dependency and screaming out for validation kick in. So then the common pattern starts – needing to get out to walk around town, appearing confident, eating in fancy restaurants – all that I cannot afford. Nothing like living on credit and loans, all to create the illusion that I am someone in society. Bloody hell, all I wanted was to make a coffee to help me focus on what I am supposed to be doing and look where my dark mind has taken me!

The handwritten envelopes addressed to me scare me the most. Those give the realisation of someone being personal to me. The fact that someone has taken the time to actually write and put thought into reaching out to me is terrifying. I can see such an addressed envelope as I look over to the pile of letters. Just peaking out from the standard service charge reminders, I can make out a white envelope with blue ink and my name spelt out in full:

'FOR ATTENTION: MR HUGO JENSEN', and the words 'PRIVATE AND CONFIDENTIAL' across the top right-hand corner.

My mind automatically attaches to the negative outcome and I feel that I will always attract the bad in my life. As they say, the universe gives what I project; so if I project negativity, all I will get is the negative. Being a freelance art historical researcher does not give me much hope for positivity these days regarding income or work. All I ever open is rejection letters for research work that I have tried to do for people or outstanding memberships that I have stopped paying. Like the memberships that I thought I would benefit from. But then I quickly understood that I had to use these to network with other members, but how does someone with insecurity and co-dependency issues with a fear of attachment actually network with people?

I will have to open these letters at some stage. I may as well open this handwritten one first as it has got my attention now. The handwriting is very delicate and elegant; it has an italic slant to it and has perfect spacing and alignment. The postal frank is difficult to view clearly to give me an indication of the postal office. Then again, who am I kidding? I have no idea how the postal franks work anyway. At least it is from the UK.

As I pull out the letter, I can see that it is cream in colour and tell that it is a weighted paper. No one writes like this in this day and age. It's a single sheet of paper. I unfold it and walk over to the balcony to read the contents.

'Dear Mr Hugo Jensen,

I trust this reaches you well and please forgive us for reaching out in this manner. It would have been more appropriate and polite to have tried to get your attention by other means of communication, such as telephone or, indeed, in person. However, it was deemed that this first contact would be much better in this written form.

We are very much interested in your research and ability to look under the surface of certain aspects with the history of art. In particular, the history of Vincent van Gogh.

We would like the opportunity to meet with you, in person, at a time and location that you feel comfortable with. We do understand that you may be particular in how and where you want to meet and we would be more than accommodating in your request. Of course, you will be remunerated for your time on all aspects.

We would eternally be grateful for your consideration to meet with us, at your earliest convenience. Please do make note of the contact details at the foot of this letter and we will be awaiting your contact.

Humbly yours,'

Well, umm, what the fuck was that all about? I need to read this again, just in case I read anything out of context or I am making up something that is not there. Why am I holding onto my breath? My chest hurts. Damn, it's the coffee; I drank it all in one gulp. Could this be a wind-up? I don't know. The language of the letter and the phrases used seem too elaborate to be a wind-up. Too much effort has been put into this. Also, hardly anyone, actually, knows of my obsessive nature of stalking the life of Vincent van Gogh. Apart from the bookstores around town. But I rotate around town with the stores so no one would ever notice plain me.

The click of the novelty date/time clock gets my attention. Fuck, it's already midday. My bloody procrastinating mood always creeps into the afternoon and, before I know it, the morning has flown by. Another 12 hours at least until I have to think about getting into that bed and reminding myself of the dark hole of being alone and needing so much to be co-dependent with someone to keep me safe. That can wait till later. I need to get to the gallery for my allocated visit time.

I must remember to discuss with Fiona why I get slightly happy and feel safe when I plan to leave the apartment for the day. Even if it is being in the chaos of London. But then, when I get there, it just reinforces that I want to share all this with someone. But then... fuck, my mind is racing again. Enough.

Where did I leave the book I am reading? That's strange. I always leave it on the hallway counter by the door, so I never forget to pick it up on the way out. It's my safety token to keep me focused on the tube. I am sure I had it yesterday on my way in. Damn, where is it? I can't go without having a book. Fuck, fuck; I can feel my heart starting to do that ache thing. Don't worry, I will begin another one, but I can't do that. It's not perfect if a book is not finished. How can I do that? It is just not the order things are done. No, no, no; I am hyperventilating. I can feel the sweat beads gathering on my forehead. I cannot disrespect the book. I need to find it and finish it. Wait, what's that orange flame of a cover I see poking out from under the newspapers? Yes. It's the book. Thank you universe.

So thankful for the Jubilee tube line. It is seldom busy and I often get a seat. I have at least 15 minutes to get back into this book, *Love in the Time of Cholera*. Great translation of the masterpiece in timeless heartbreak; I love storytelling by Gabriel Márquez. It is a good break from the normal dark, suspenseful genre I usually go for. Maybe it will get me to look at life with a bit more hope and positivity. Next is to change my Spotify playlist to get out of the sad, emotive genre.

Still unable to get that letter out of my head. Do I read it again now? Let it disrupt my solitude reading time? That *was* why I brought it along with me, was it not? Why are my hands sweaty as I unfold it? It's not going to jump up and attack me. But the words and the manner of them are slightly unnerving.

It's easy to see that my research into Vincent van Gogh is of interest to them. This is evidence and it jumps off the page with direct force. The other aspects that give me the shivers are the references to 'us' and 'we'. This involves not just another individual; it's plural. Group of people or organisation or – fuck – a gang. Mobsters. Shit! Or it could just be an elderly couple in their 80s, wanting to hear some interesting facts about art.

Damn, what station was that we just passed? I must be close to my stop. I am sure it was Waterloo. The walk up from Westminster station to the National Gallery will only take me about five minutes or so. I am sure the next stop is mine.

The letter also mentions that they perhaps also have the means to contact me by phone or 'in person', which indicates that they have those details, including where I live. Shit. I am now being stalked. Now, I have an image of an 80-year-old couple, huddled together, sitting in some old Mini car watching me and taking notes as I leave home and arrive back during my days. The other two words that jump out at me are 'eternally' and 'Humbly'. Who uses such vocabulary in letters these days? Unless it is someone who feels I have something or know something of importance they need. They obviously have the wrong person in mind.

Why has the train stopped? Crap, this is my stop.

5

Now

I let Femi concentrate and lead the way after our little rest. I have not wanted to ask what he saw or found when he went into the bushes. He looked spooked when he returned, eyes wide and I am also sure I noticed a slight bead of sweat on his brow. The humidity is strangulating now, but I dare not ask Femi to slow down again or complain about the climate conditions. Whatever he discovered out there in the bush, it has caused him to get to the meeting point and onto that boat with urgency.

Moving along the riverbank that is cut off from all the tourist hot spots, we leave nothing to chance that anyone should spot us. The issue with that safety is that it takes us through all Luxor's natural, unpopulated and undeveloped landscape, which, with it, brings bloody insects and mosquitos and all sorts of creatures that cause rashes and bumps and itch-infested lesions all over the skin. I just know that I will be getting infective abscesses everywhere over the next few days. I am sure I read somewhere that malaria was non-existent in Egypt now, however; the River Nile still carries the extreme risk of typhoid fever, dysentery and cholera.

"We will switch once we pass that clearing just over

that mount ahead," I heard Femi say as he cleared the drooping leaves out of his path. It comes as a welcome respite as the load on my back now feels like it weighs a ton. I will just be glad to have air on my back.

"Hugo?"

"Yes, sorry; I heard. That sounds like a good plan." Something has definitely rattled him.

Femi lets the bags down to the floor once we reach the clearing.

"Turn around to slowly unbuckle and loosen the braces to create a bit of slack," Femi instructs while he stands behind me to take hold of the package on my back. "Let me know when you have released the shoulder strap buckles."

My hands are covered in sweat and tremor slightly. Must be the sugar levels dropping. I know we will have time now for some of those glucose protein bars. They are sticky and chewy as hell, but much needed. Anything tastes nice out here when the palate has not had a decent meal in ages.

"The buckles are open." I can't wait to get this off me. As the load loosens from my back, the air between the two surfaces now causes a chill to run down my spine.

"OK, I have the load and will maintain the pressure. Undo the torso buckle now and let them all fall lax."

"Sure." I sound nervous in my reply, but I want to get this off me now and ask Femi directly what occurred back there in the bush.

I can feel it peel off my back and I feel lighter now. I turn to see Femi, gentle and with intense concentration, laying the rectangular package onto the flat clearing between us.

"Let's take a few mins to catch our breath," he suggests while looking at his watch. "We have some of those protein bars in that bag," he motions with his head.

In the distance I can hear the mesmerising tones of prayer from the various mosques scattered around this terrain. I cannot see any buildings on the horizon, but from the sounds, I am sure there are some small, local settlements with speakers, allowing the Islamic call to prayer, called Adhan, to encompass the air around us.

Femi concentrates on ensuring the package is safe and secure on the ground, checking for any breach of the packaging. I can hear my stomach growling away from the hunger within it, so I turn my attention to the bag with the bars.

"What flavour do you want?" I find a selection of chocolate or vanilla and strawberry. Not that any of them taste any different. Femi does not answer. I turn to see him sitting on the ground with his knees drawn up and hands over his head. At first, I thought he was praying, but then I can see he looks deep in thought on closer inspection. "Femi…"

"What!" His answer is more of a shout. "Sorry, I was miles away. What is it?"

"I… I was just asking, what flavour do you want to have of these protein bars?"

"Any, it doesn't matter. They all taste like crap anyway."

Femi tenses his jawline while answering. I never asked him how he got that scar on the right side of his face. It becomes so pronounced when he tightens his jaw muscles and his temporal area. It has a crescent moon shape to it, starting from just lateral to his eye and coming down in a smooth arch to the corner of his mouth on the right side. When he tenses his facial muscles, the deep indentations of the scar come to the surface. You can make out where the overlaying skin tissue has been folded over on itself, to reduce the width of the cut and allow the two edges to knit together. I assume it is a scar inflicted upon him and not present from birth. Perhaps an altercation of some sort or an accident resulting from a fall. Whatever caused it, he has not mentioned it in any story to date and I have not asked either.

"You can have the chocolate," I say while throwing a bar over to him. He watches, eyes fixed on me, but not following the flying object. He doesn't make any effort to catch it. It lands at his feet. I cannot help but feel slightly anxious now. He is supposed to be in control and make sure I feel secure here. All this is going to do is make my irrational thought processes race and make all sorts of inferences. Obviously, I will take this as a personal attack on me of some sort. Maybe he has lost interest in the quest and me. Maybe he feels this is not worth all the trouble. Maybe he feels *I* am not worth all the trouble. What if he thinks I am worthless and a fake? Everything I am doing is a fake; what if that is what he has come to realise? No, please not him also. I trusted him; I need him to be true with me, here and now. Please do not let him be like all those others in London. All those others who got fed up with me and moved on after I let them see the real me. How I think back to how she, that woman, undressed me to the naked me in public. How she let her venom out on me. Spat it all out and told me how worthless I was. How everything I have attained was all-pathetic and, underneath it all, I was nobody with nothing. How I recall the look in her eyes and the smile she showed when she told me I would always be alone and would never be a father. How could she? How could she pick the one thing that I lived for, to be a father, and tear that dream away from my inner protection? Please, Femi, not you as well – not now. I need someone to be true to me for once.

"Femi!" My voice is shaky as I call his name. At the sound of his name, it is like he comes alive again, a spell being broken. His eyes blink and narrow to focus on me. He reaches for the bar at his feet.

"Thank you, Hugo. Sorry. I was just…"

He stops mid-sentence.

The air is suddenly still around us. The speakers are silent from the nearby settlements.

"Femi. What happened back there? What did you discover in the bushes?" I need to know what has rocked his concentration.

He did not look up at me. Just sat there, studying the protein bar in his hands, passing it from one hand to the other. He made the bar look like a matchstick in his giant hands.

"Femi!"

He stopped toying with the bar and let it fall to the floor between his legs.

"It's nothing. I guess I just felt a little anxious to get this package, and us, safely to Cairo."

I don't believe him. I look directly at him, not letting my intense stare subside, as I require a more substantial answer. I knew he knew I was looking at him and he avoided looking up at me.

"Look…" I decided to take the lead and be the confident one here now. "This is shit, this whole situation we are in, but you said to leave the protective aspects to you." I waited to allow him to give some sort of response. Still nothing. Maybe he was praying and I should back off. "But that also means that we need to communicate to make sure we are both on the same page and not add to the fucking anxiety here."

That sentence on communication takes me back to the issue with *her*. *"We need to communicate better and be open and understanding of each other."* Those were her exact words. Fucking idiot I was to fall for that old excuse. More like communicate better to allow her to fucking use me. Shit, no, stop. Where is my mind going? Must be the heat. That is not what she did. I knew we needed some sort of resolution or closure with each other. Now I am sitting here with this overgrown man who obviously needs to be in some sort of Ridley Scott *Gladiator* film, in charge of my life, and I am thinking back to her and the pathetic way we navigated our so-called relationship. I need to make a mental note to discuss with Fiona when I get back to London how to create closure with that.

Femi's watch bleeps in a sequence of quick-fire beeps. It brings me back to us here. I realise I have hardly had any of my protein bar, so I take a couple of big bites and fill my mouth. The crumbs spill out. It takes an eternity to chew this damn thing and now I wish I had not taken such large chunks. Femi still has not touched his.

He lets out a sigh and finally acknowledges me with his eyes. His head is still sunken into his shoulders. He looks dejected.

"Hugo, everything is OK. It will be much easier once we get to my cousin's and we are on the boat sailing up the Nile."

This was the first time I did not believe him totally. Fuck. This is just what I need, not trusting someone I literally depend on now, for my life.

"Come. Let's get the inspection of the package done and safely secure it on my back. We need to keep up the pace we have set," Femi says while he puts the unopened protein bar in his cargo pants pocket and stands up.

"Fine, don't share your concerns with me," I think to myself. *"But don't come crying to me when I push you away and your name joins the long list of people who have abandoned me in the past."*

"Yeh, sure. You are right, Femi. We need to keep the pace we have set." And, as if it is a pantomime, there is the high-pitched cry of some exotic bird from a distance, as our cue for the next act.

6

Before

"Hi, I am about 20 minutes late for my allocated visiting time." Gosh, I am breathless from the brisk walk from Westminster tube station to the National Galley, right on the steps of Trafalgar Square.

"Do you have your electronic ticket?" comes the indifferent response from the entrance's security guard. I am conscious of the line of people behind me, trying to keep warm in the cold.

I fumble with my gloves to pull my phone out of my coat pocket. Damn gloves. I whip one off out of frustration and I am sure this guy standing here like some sort of gatekeeper is enjoying my anguish at this episode.

"Here you go; knew it was here somewhere on the phone," I respond, letting out a slightly nervous chuckle. He doesn't look very impressed. He just waves his hand in the direction of the doors behind him, indicating I can pass.

I know exactly where I want to go. I always feel calm in galleries. I identify with the art. With the individuals who created such pieces. They are artefacts that capture the history and emotion experienced at that time. As with all beautiful works of achievement, they often come from a place of pain and torment. I can resonate so much in that aspect. Not that I have ever created great works of art or great works of anything for that matter, but the emotional rollercoaster is all the same.

Route C is the one I need to take. To room 41. That is my only destination today. How many times I have done this same thing. I've come here and sat in room 41 opposite the rectangular object hung on the wall and suspended with metal rod chains from the coving high above.

It is not too busy here midweek, which is a blessing. The worst is when I misjudge it and end up amongst a busy, noisy, disruptive group of school kids. But today, just well behaved people. Elegant and appropriate.

Route C would normally take 25 minutes to complete if one took time looking at all the aspects on offer. I cannot recall when I have actually just come here and taken in all the art without coming here for my own research aspects. Then again, my research aspects have not given me any means of income so far. I worry if it has become an unhealthy obsession. On the way to room 41, the first room lays the foundation for the characteristic theme that runs throughout the gallery. Wooden herringbone pattern flooring and floral wallpaper that I can only imagine has a velvet touch to it. Domed ceilings with gold leaf reef patterns across the perimeter. I always find it fascinating how the green rope, draped to the edge of the rooms, is intended to keep people away from physically manhandling the artwork. I have been so tempted to push the boundaries and reach out and touch the canvas. To feel the ridges of the paint edges. To be part of that time, when it was created. To wish I could somehow have history also understand my battles within my own mind. Perhaps that is why I empathise with the artists here. Perhaps I see a reflection of myself in the paintings, as often, as mentioned earlier, such artists suffer with their own demons and use the art as therapy and expressionism.

Without stopping to view the many great works present, I continue walking through. The central room has three great arched doorways with the name, 'ROTHSCHILD', engraved in the coving overhead in gold lettering. I need to remind myself to look more into that. I make a mental note of this every time I come here, but never remember to see the link with Rothschild and this place. I suppose I have enough obsessive investigative compulsions at present to keep my mind fixated.

I am sure I recognise some of the same security guards here. I am convinced that the CCTV cameras use facial recognition now to alert everyone that I am back again. God forbid that there is actually a break in here or something goes missing. I would be the prime number one suspect. To make matters worse, the uncomfortable attention to and explanations I would need to provide when asked why I am drawing plans of the layouts of the rooms and paintings on the walls. I suppose I may make some money from the attention of being falsely accused. I can just see the headlines now: 'Burn out – has-been journalist steals priceless artwork'. I could even write the article for the papers.

What an odd-looking gentleman. Crossing my path, as I walk into the grand central hallway opening. This section's rooms are my favourite part here. The flooring is marble and the domed glass ceiling is reminiscent of basilicas in Rome. This guy seems so out of place here. Not sure with regard to location, but in time. He has the flair of someone back in the 1920s. He must be in his 80s. Has a swift gait, but with a slight limp to his right leg or hip. But in any case, he still moves pretty quickly and confidently. Wearing a pinstripe, grey three-piece suit. A long tailcoat with three white buttons along the central back tail. A bowler hat that creates even more suspense to him as the rim provides shade over his forehead. Two-tone jazz/tap-type shoes and a white rose pinned to his right lapel to finish things off. Bizarre, to say the least, but nice to see and to break up people's normality. It seems he is going in the same direction as me. As he turned right, he entered The Sackler Room, which leads to room 41. Wait... fuck! What was I thinking, about a couple in their 80s writing me that letter? No, it can't be. My imagination is running overtime. He is just here to enjoy the displays – if he wants to dress as elegant as that, well, good for him.

I can instinctively tell that most people going into room 41 will be gravitating towards the painting that I want to study again. I must know this painting so intimately by now – each inch, each perfect brush stroke. The delicate weaves of paint and direction creating a masterpiece when you view it from the far end of the room. But up close, up right near the surface, next to the energy of the individual layers and thread by thread, gives the artist protection behind the surface. And I was not wrong. As I walk into room 41, it opens up into a square room; two dark mahogany benches sit in the middle of the room. Overhead lights suspended from wires and rods from the walls and ceiling create the lighting. The lighting has never done justice to the paintings in here. They always give such a matt, dull ambience to the work.

To the left, as I enter the room, I see the huddle of people around the masterpiece. Well, that is not a fair comment. These are *all* masterpieces. But one in particular is better well known than the others. To the wall on the left, five paintings hang, also suspended by the chains from the overhead coving. The second painting in the corner of the room is where all the attention is focused.

The same spot on the opposite wall is where the security guard sits. Every so often he is watching, waiting to jump into action. Itching to use the walkie-talkie and to call for backup. Damn, my back feels drenched with sweat from the layers I am wearing. I have all day. I can take my time. There are still some aspects of the colour textures and blending that puzzle me. Each time I come, I look for hidden clues and answers, but in reality, maybe I am just being a lost romantic as there is no great mystery to how the colours were chosen or blended to create the painting. But, how have they ended up being so perfect from the painter who had issues processing and interpreting colour compared to how 'normal' people do? Again, more fascination in fuelling my obsession with him.

I do not need to listen to the audio tour that accompanies this room or go up close to read the label next to the painting. I have gathered enough information over the years to give a fully comprehensive lecture on the painting and the artist. I feel a shadow creeping up over my shoulder and, as ever, the vigilant guard has left his post of the chair to move by my side. As he walks past, I can see the name tag 'Emilio'. I like that name. Kind and soft in nature.

The crowd is clearing from the item of desire; just for me it seems. For the first time, I also note how calm and at ease with myself I am since coming into this room.

This is therapy for me. This is when all my darkness is locked away and unable to breach the walls. This is my place of safety, my inner temple of solace. I catch a glimpse of the painting. I have a clear line of sight now. Oil on canvas painting, dating to 1888, measuring 92.1cm x 73cm. The fourth version of *Sunflowers* by Vincent van Gogh.

7

Before

"So, tell me where your fascination with Vincent van Gogh festered from." My Thursday afternoon psychotherapy session with Fiona starts with an ice-breaker. Well, there never is a real ice-breaker with Fiona. She is a brilliant individual and I am more than aware that she knows what my emotion is the moment I walk into the room.

"Well, it's not really a fascination. That could be misconstrued as an obsession. It's more of an interest." I notice I am always defensive at the start of each session. Like needing to somehow balance the power in this territory of hers. But it always fails. I am soon reminded that this is a safe space and there is no need for me to have barriers and walls up. Even though I have been coming to see Fiona for three years now, or is it four? Bloody hell, it could be five if we count that break when I was convinced that I was 'fixed'. Well, anyway, all these years, I still feel anxious for the first few minutes of the session to not let Fiona down. She can recognise the pattern I have and just waits for me to settle into the corner of the sofa, gradually relax my shoulders and allow my hands to fall by my side as opposed to them covering my mouth as a defence mechanism.

"I just find the history and torment of the man to be such a tragic story as he was a hopeless romantic. There was so much that he battled with. Within himself. It must have been a daily struggle with his mind of enormous magnitude." Fuck. The penny just dropped. I know where Fiona is going with this. I can feel my shoulders tense up again and I sit up a little straighter on the sofa. The sun reflects off the windows from the buildings across the street and right into my eyes.

"Do you mind if we pull the blinds down a bit?" I ask. "The sun is right in my eyes." I am glad I can create a bit of distraction here. I feel the nervousness rising and a bead of sweat developing on my forehead. By now, Fiona knows all my tricks to allow myself to take the attention off a bit. The temperature in the room, the noise outside, the light shining through, the new books on the shelves... Has Fiona done something different to her hair? How is it out in the sticks where Fiona lives? But, whatever I say, she sees right through it and, as always, with delicate navigation, brings me back to the much-needed train of thought.

"Is that better for you?" she asks after pulling the blind down and sitting back in her chair opposite me.

"Thank you. Now at least I can see you."

"So... You were saying about van Gogh battling with his mind."

She is not going to let me get away with this today, is she?

"His paintings had a combination of his real passion for art and also how he used his art to reflect his torn emotions." Fuck it, let's see where this goes and what conclusions Fiona can make from my rambles.

She sits there, focused on my posture. Looking for any

clues that may unravel my mind as I speak my words.

"I mean…. It is no secret that a person who cuts off his own ear would obviously have some aspect of mental health concerns." I notice Fiona shift forward slightly in her seat and I need to reassure her before she concludes what I think she is going to conclude. "Do not worry. I am not having any self-harm ideation or intent." I get a gentle smile back.

"Well, I suppose it was not in the actual act of cutting his own ear off, but what led him to it and what made him deliver the ear to where he left it." Of course, Fiona would know more about van Gogh than I would. Is there anything she does *not* know? She continues, as she always does, to get me to come out of my shell and give my inner thoughts.

"What do you think he was trying to communicate out to the world, Hugo?"

I know what I want to say. But I also know that perhaps similar traits may leak my inner monster out here.

"You mean, why he cut his ear off or why he delivered it to a local prostitute?" I push the question right back at her. Two can play at this game. Crap, she doesn't take the bait and just leans back and smiles, not taking her eyes off me. I know she wants me to take the lead; it is my therapy session after all.

I take a deep breath, close my eyes and put my hand over my neck, rubbing it. This is when I know I feel that someone can see through me. As I open my eyes, I feel I need to get this out. At times, it is easier to speak in the second or third person, to try and get my emotions out. And who better than to use Vincent van Gogh as one of my characters?

"Well, he was constantly in battle within himself. He struggled with acceptance and how he saw his own perfections that were imperfections in his own eyes. As he wrote once to his brother, 'I dream what I will paint and then I paint my dream', which basically says that the world will see his mind, dreams, hopes and fears from his paintings. This was a brave step for him to admit out to the world."

Fiona seems genuinely interested in what I am saying. I know she will come back to the dream comment I just mentioned. I can put money on it. I continue.

"One of his friends, a very accomplished painter, was coming to stay with him. In preparation, Vincent drew his sunflowers to decorate the rooms. What transpired was that there were several different points of opinion on the paintings and the techniques used. The climax was an argument that resulted in Vincent cutting his own ear off."

There was a hum from Fiona. "So, he cut his ear off in anger or protest of the difference of opinions on their craft?" she asks.

"No. Not at all. It was not in anger *or* protest. This is how it has been interpreted, but it was a beautiful act of love and thankfulness."

I think I have Fiona stumped, for once. She frowns and asks,

"Sorry, I don't understand. 'Love and thankfulness'."

"Well, yes; he spends weeks getting ready for his friend to visit. He was anxious to impress this other artist. He felt like a child, being excited and wanting to make this person proud. Again, he writes such passages in the weeks leading up to the visit in letters to his brother. Vincent was experiencing feelings of wanting to make sure everything was perfect. He wanted to make the visit safe and meaningful for both, so he tried to create something that represented his dreams at that time. Sunflowers. Bright, showing hope. Needing natural light and love before the flowers faded away. Vincent needed to be the caregiver for the flowers, to paint them in their perfect natural form."

I pause to be sure Fiona is following. And then she says what I was expecting her to say.

"So, he created a co-dependent form of dynamics between himself and the sunflowers."

I nod and continue. "It was a beautifully high, happy time for him in those days leading up to the visit. His dreams were reflected on the canvas and he was letting someone in. He was allowing the trust to show this to someone, in an intimate setting, in his own house. But…" I sigh before continuing, "…with every high comes the biggest crash."

I can feel myself starting to see my own reflection in this. I have to be conscious not to say the word 'I' when speaking now, as this has a direct route back to my own torment.

"When his friend arrived, and in the coming days, they discussed various painting techniques and the contrast between the two artists – Vincent saw it as direct criticism."

Fuck, I can feel the frog in my throat. Just hold it in, take a moment and breathe. She will understand.

"I suppose he then saw his friend as someone who would see his imperfections. Someone who came there with pretence to care, to share, but after all, someone who would belittle and abandon him. But this is the spiral that Vincent got into. There was no reasoning with his inner self when he got like that. He would then turn to impulse behaviours, which defied all levels of appropriateness and boundaries. The inner wounded child came out. He felt that if he got to show an act of real sacrifice to this friend, it would win back the respect and admiration and he would not abandon him. He could not give his life; he needed his eyes and hands to paint, so he chose his ear. A part of him to make a statement: I am hurt, I need you, I want you to see me as perfect, I want you to validate me as I cannot validate myself."

I stop. I realise that I was speaking without much pause for breath. There is silence filling the space between us.

"Well, that is certainly a powerful act and viewpoint of his actions. I suppose I never even thought of it in that way."

Umm, I think I impressed her.

"Now. Tell me, Hugo, what do you think his dreams tell us?"

Fuck, I knew it.

8

Now

"How do you think we are doing for time and distance?" I shout to Femi up ahead. We are now much closer to the river. It's just over the ridge to our right. The sound of the water crashing gently on the shore as the boats pass gives me a calming emotion. It takes me back again to the balcony at home. It was always so much better when she would sit with me, side by side, legs all over each other on the balcony, late at night.

"We are close. Maybe another hour or so." Femi was not breathless at all, even with the added extra weight on his back of the package.

I was hoping he would get the hint that I want water or a break just to take these fucking heavy boots off. They are getting on my nerves now. So bloody warm and too insulating. The air remains humid and everything just sticks to every aspect of my skin. There are only so many times I can lick my dry chapped lips, but that just enhances the process of drying them further. Femi continues to clear the path of bushes ahead. The dense is clearing the closer we get to the shore, now. Not sure if that is a good thing for our cover. If we truly are being followed, then we are getting more and more out in the open.

I see Femi suddenly stop moving and stand up straight. Fuck, has he seen something? I stop a couple of feet behind him. I use the time to clear the sweat off my face and pull my top away from my drenched, salty skin.

"What's wrong?" I voice, just above a whisper.

Femi turns to face me.

"Nothing." He sighs. His eyes look softer than I have seen them. Maybe he does get tired after all. "Let's take a few minutes to sit and catch our breath." This is a nice surprise suggestion from him.

"Sounds good to me. I need to take these boots off for a while."

I move to Femi as he turns around to take the package off his back. This is out of normal protocol, but I am sure Femi has this all under control. Once we have secured the package on the floor so it is flat and out of harm's way, we both find a spot to sit. There is no shade here as the bush is quite flat now, so I take a t-shirt out of the bag to put over my head to create some protection from the sun.

Femi takes a bottle of water out, has a couple of big gulps and hands it over to me.

"What happened to you guys?" The question catches me off-guard. I stop halfway with my sip of water. The bottle sticks in-between my lips and I glance sideways at Femi.

"What do you mean?" I know exactly what Femi is asking.

"When we were in London. I could tell you had someone in your life. It was obvious from your actions and your…" He stalls. I can tell he is finding the gentler way of putting this across to me. "…Well, you just seemed so heartbroken. Even when you were in the midst of finding one of the world's most valuable artefacts that had been assumed missing, you still seemed just so distracted by something, someone. And there is only one thing that does that to a man."

What the hell! Was it that obvious? Now I don't know what to feel. To feel that Femi really has traits of friendship and empathy towards me or to feel pathetic that it was obvious I was coming off the downslope of yet another failed relationship. Thinking back now, I suppose everything was just happening all at once back in London. My freelance journalist work was going nowhere fast but down a black hole. My finances were a mess. And yes, the woman who I was and still am deeply in love with, had had enough of me, had left and moved on. Pretty quickly moved on, mind you.

"What are you, some relationship coach or something?" My statement/question was spat back towards Femi, not intentionally. I suppose it was more of a reflective and defensive stance of mine. As soon as the words left my lips, I bit down on my tongue and tried to remember what Fiona had taught me about allowing people in, just enough – with boundaries – but not to snap too soon, as not everyone is out to use and hurt me. "Sorry. I didn't mean to sound flippant. It's just a long story."

"Well, we are lumbered together for a while, unfortunately. And I suppose I need a happy/sad love story to remind me of my own family."

This is the first time Femi has referenced aspects of his family. I never quizzed him in the past. I know of his approximate village and where he grew up, but as to what his life is like now, it feels too personal and, perhaps, too hurtful to go into.

I almost forget where we are. I look around me briefly to remind me of our surroundings. The sun is coming down with a purpose now. Everything is still. No leaves moving at all. The sky is clear blue with not even a whisper of a cloud present. Femi is still just to my left, a few feet ahead. His right leg is stretched out in front of him with his left leg bent up at the knee and he's holding onto it with his arms. He is looking straight at me in anticipation of my story. Something about his presence, energy and karma gives me a slight notation that I can trust him.

I give in and start to give him some details.

"It just got so complicated." What is the worst he can do, laugh at me? Tell me to move on and that there are plenty more fish in the sea? "It was a chance meeting. It was actually over a painting. It was back in the summer last year. There was a van Gogh exhibition taking place in the grounds of Somerset House. I was there just to take in the atmosphere rather than to learn anything new. It was more of a commercial exhibition."

I can feel my inner adrenaline start to build. I know this is not the safe room that Fiona provides. That is thousands of miles away right now. Suddenly, I want to shift my posture, but it is difficult to hide from Femi while out here in the open.

"Well, that sounds like a promising start, both liking art."

I chuckle slightly at Femi's sentence.

"Well, you would think, hey. But she wasn't there for the art." Femi checks his watch. "Do we have to get going?" I ask.

"No, no; not at all." Femi motions for the water bottle from me. "We have more time than I thought. We have made really good time."

Damn. He wants me to talk. I can always set a boundary and say I do not want to share. But, I am sure I trust him. I am sure I feel safe with him.

"You were saying how you met this woman…"

I hesitate to mention any names. It always feels easier when not attaching a name.

"There was a display of some of the letters van Gogh had written to his brother, at one of the stands. I was there, just glancing over them. Most of the attention was on the digital painting displays, so this stand was pretty much secluded."

I pause as I picture the scene and recall our conversation back there on that day…

"Excuse me." Her voice was so gentle and sweet. I looked up and saw what I could only explain as near to an angel as I have ever seen.

"Sorry, did I disturb you?" Her voice again.

"Hi, yes, sorry. No, no; not at all. How can I help? Am I in your way? Do you want to look at the display?" My words came out rushed and fucking stupid. I had a couple of books under my arm and my mobile foldaway keyboard in my right hand. I suddenly felt like such a boring dork standing here in front of this lady. She was wearing a white summer dress that fell just above her knees. The bottom had a slight angle cut to it, with a central slip elegantly folded over it and held together with a belt across her waist. Her blonde hair fell just below her shoulders. Slightly curly in nature. Then I noticed a flower wreath on her head. There were pink and white flowers all around the circumference of her head. She must have noticed me looking slightly perplexed at this.

"The flowers, right," she commented in a shy yet confident manner. She smiled and reached up to touch the flowers on her head. "It's midsummer's day today – June 26th. It's when we celebrate the summer solstice."

"'We'?"

"Yep, it's a national tradition in Sweden."

I should have known. The glowing skin, the intense green eyes and the flowing blonde hair. She was from Sweden.

"Well, they suit you." So fucking dumb. I didn't know what to say. Then I remembered she had wanted to ask me something. "Sorry, you wanted to ask something."

"Oh yes, it looks like you work here." She glanced down at the books under my arm. Both had references to van Gogh on them. Great – I thought she was actually interested in me.

"I am looking for the Spring Restaurant. It is supposed to be somewhere here, but this is a maze. Would you know how I could get to it, please?"

"Sure. It's over the courtyard down that corridor that leads straight to it." I gestured the direction with my head, as I was conscious of the sweat patches potentially developing under my armpits, both from the day's heat and due to me freaking out standing here talking to this person.

She smiled again and thanked me with that sweet voice and walked in the direction that I had indicated.

I look back at Femi to see if he is still following. His focus is so deep and on what I had previously said. It's like he has forgotten what our mission is. When he notices me looking back at him, he asks,

"So, was that how you met the woman that broke your heart?"

I take a deep breath and look away.

"No, Femi. That was the woman whose heart *I* broke."

We let those words sit there in the air between us. The soft inviting sounds of the shoreline the only welcome disturbance.

"It seems this is indeed a complex story to tell. A story perhaps we need to leave for another time," Femi suggests. He gets up and dusts the grass off his cargo pants. "Come, we need to get this strapped back onto me." He holds his arm out to me and pulls me off the ground. "Hugo." He looks straight into my eyes. He stands a good few inches above me. The sun is directly behind him, high in the sky, but he creates enough shade to allow me to look at him. "You are a good man. Remember that. Always."

There is a moment, just for a couple of seconds, where I think he wants to say something more. But he doesn't.

9

Before

'Creativity and chronic disease in Vincent van Gogh'. What an imaginative title for a paper written by a clinical professor of pathology on the various theories of what was going on with the great painter. I don't think I have slept for five nights in a row. Normally, I would get a couple of hours here and there, but the last five days have been torture. Maybe I am at risk of becoming manic with my thinking now. Every time I try and just switch off, my mind races. Tonight, I have been searching through every corner of the Internet for corners of Vincent van Gogh that I have not yet discovered.

My eyes ache and I can feel the heavy swelling under each of them. I dare not even look in the mirror, as I do not want to see how ugly and wasted-looking I have become. The more I try to use reading or meditation to get into a place of mindfulness, the more I need to focus on the traumas. My memory is also really starting to frighten me now. I am starting to recall darkness from many years ago, yet some facts of recent years I am blanking out. I only saw Fiona a few days ago, but I struggle to remember my homework. I think it was to try to visualise thoughts in black and white so that I can minimise their impact. I think that is what it was.

Back to focusing on this paper. I narrow my eyes to read the small font. I am too lethargic to try and turn the other lights on. The switch seems so far away, over there on the wall. 'Manic depression' and 'epilepsy' are two of the diagnoses that float around in this paper to summarise Vincent's mental capacity. Then, to explain his love of the colour yellow, it is suggested that he had taken high doses of *Digitalis purpurea*, which is the purple or common foxglove from which the drug is extracted. To treat his epilepsy. This could have accounted for his visual colour defect.

It is so easy for people to judge aspects of mood disturbance when they will never totally understand the burden one goes through. Poor Vincent. I got you, man.

Ummm, I suppose it can't hurt. Just a little drink, just a small whisky to try to get the brain cells to switch off. I mean, strictly speaking, alcohol is not a medication issued to help me sleep; therefore, I am in control of it. Fiona does not need to know that I may have been trying to use it to help get me to count sheep in my bed. Damn, its 3.56 AM, according to my phone. How did the hours slip by?

Was my sleep this bad before *her*? I don't think it was. It was never great, but now it's just a total mess. But since she left, since I made her leave, my days and nights have been a never-ending clash of a mirage of each other.

I will try the single malt Port Charlotte whisky this evening. It's been sitting there ready for me for the last few weeks. *"Cheers, Vincent. To all the fucked up, tormented, misunderstood bastards in the world."*

What... No! Really? Why is the bottle only a little full now? And how did I end up on the floor in the kitchen? I thought I was in the bedroom with the drink. Is it morning already? Fuck, so confused or is it bedtime? The room spinning or is it my head? Or both. Wow! Easy… Better not try and get up just yet.

"I suggest you stay sitting there for a bit, on the floor."

What the hell!

"Hello? Who is there?"

"You know who I am. Stop playing about with me. You know very well who I am."

I recognise the voice. But how?

"How did you get in? Wh-what are you doing back here?" I know that voice anywhere. That sweet innocence and happiness in the tone. The joy from her voice.

"Oh dear. You are such a silly man. I never left. Why would I?"

Could this be real? Everything is spinning so much.

"Where are you?"

"I am here, my dear. I will always be here with you. Regardless of how you treated me."

No, no. This is just a dream. I can feel the bile coming up to hit the back of my throat.

"I can't see you…" I try to focus my eyes on the open-plan lounge and dining room as I sit on the floor in the kitchen, like a small child. The rest of the space is in darkness around me. The only light source is the overhead extractor fan above the electric cooker that has spotlights on it. They shine down directly over me.

"Do you really need to see me, my dear? I am sure you remember my beauty. It should be tattooed on your brain."

Her voice is losing its softness now. I try again to bend my knees and stand by pushing off my hands. But it's no use. Everything just seems so unstable.

"I know I am dreaming. You are not really here."

I hear her laugh. That cute laugh always followed by a little snort at the end. I think the cause of her snort was due to her extremely narrow nostrils. She used to dare me to try to widen them by putting my fingers up them. I never knew adults could have such narrow nostrils. That would explain her snoring.

"If I am not here, then whom are you talking to? Whose voice are you listening to?"

That was a fair point from her.

"How did you get in? I thought I took the keys back." I can sense my own words slurring as I try to get them out as coherently as I can.

The light shining down on me makes it difficult to look up. My eyes squint again as I try to find where her voice is coming from. She must be sitting on the far end of the sofa.

"Hello. Are you still there?" The room is in silence again. I can hear the low rumble of the fridge over to my right. My mind flicks over to the inside of the fridge. Empty, as always.

"How could you?" I hear her voice again. More determined in its tone now. I can feel the bile hitting the back of my throat again as I try to reply.

"Ho-how... what? How could I, what?"

I hear a tut. Or was that the sound of the clock ticking over again?

"You put me through so much shit. What did I ever do to you to make you hate me so much?"

I try again to look over to the back of the sofa to see if I can see her. "Please. Please help me up so we can talk."

"Why should I? Why did you torture me all that time? All I ever did was want to care for you. To be there for you.

To hold your hand through it. Why? Tell me, Hugo. Why did you turn to hate me so much, my dear?"

The sound of my name makes me feel slightly nauseous. The room is spinning more now. I can feel myself slowly lean to my right and reach the floor. I lay my head on the wooden flooring. My eyes are focused on the back of the sofa from a low eye level and it looks like a mountain ridge. I blink. My eyelids are heavy and tired again.

"I… I never hated you. I did not know how to—"

"What, Hugo? You did not know how to what, Hugo?"

I know what I want to say. But my brain doesn't seem to want my mouth to move.

"Just like I thought. You have not changed. Still not willing to speak up and be a man. Pathetic."

No. No. This cannot happen again. She is devaluing me. But do I deserve it? Did I really cause that much hate and pain towards her? I did not know I was doing it. It was the monster in me that came out.

"It wasn't me, I mean…" Fuck, I can hear my words back at me. I *do* sound pathetic. "I mean, I didn't recognise my behaviour at the time and I understand now they were not justified or right. For that I have never been able to do or say anything to take that back from you."

I do not know if anything I am saying makes any sense.

"I tried so much with you, Hugo. I was patient. I was tolerant of your moods. Of you constantly pushing me away. I even tried to understand why you directed your insecurities onto me."

I close my eyes and curl up on the floor like a wounded child. Through my t-shirt, I can feel how cold the floor is. As I reopen my eyes, I can just see the slight dim light coming in from outside the balcony, reaching over the sofa. I am sure I just saw a flash of lightning.

"You made me a person who was not me. You drained everything from me. My inner beauty was destroyed because of you."

Her voice contains so much hate. She spits the words out. I open my mouth to form a reply, but all I can muster is a pathetic aspect of drool from the corner of my mouth, which falls onto the floor and comes to rest under my cheek.

"I know. And I wish I could cut all ties with how I was back then. But I cannot. I have to take responsibility for my actions." These words seem so repetitive now. When all I want to do is scream that I fucked up because I am a mess, but it is not my choice. It was and it is not something that I planned. What I want to do is stand up and shout that I am broken. That I have been broken for as long as I can remember.

"You knew what you were doing, my dear. You are too clever to act like you had no idea of your actions."

She never will understand the inner chaos of my mind. No matter what I do or say.

I can see a dark shadow move above the back of the sofa. I can make out her head and her hair tied high in a ponytail. I always found her so beautiful when she tied her hair up like that. The silhouette is striking. Her long, slender neck as she looks to the side. She reaches up with her arms to stretch. Slowly, she moves closer to me, shifting on the sofa.

"Do you miss me, my dear?"

He voice now soft and tender. I do not know how to reply. I want to tell her that I want to love her, but I don't know how. I blink. I now notice the light above me has been turned off. When did that happen or was it off the whole time? Now, in the blackness, I see her move closer to me. The outline of her body now reminding me of what she was. I can tell she is climbing over the back of the sofa to get to me. My eyes blink in a heavy, tired manner. If I only close them for a couple of seconds, just to get a bit of rest, it will help. It will let me think clearer.

In the darkness, I feel my mind spinning. Closing my eyes just made that sensation magnify. How long did I keep my eyes closed? As I open them, it takes me a few moments and repeated blinking to get my bearings again. I am still on the floor in the kitchen. The room is in darkness now. No light. Ahead of me, lying there, I can make out an outline of someone. I remember now; she was on the sofa and then came to lay on the floor with me.

"You came back to me."

There was no reply from her. Just absolute stillness to the figure. My vision starts to clear. I can focus better now. The outline doesn't look like her anymore.

The fridge is now silent. The low hum of it has stopped. I can hear the deep breaths of this figure in front of me. The breath sounds heavy and tired. There are only a couple of feet between us. Close enough to reach out and touch each other.

"How did you get in? Have you been here long?" Those were the only words I could think of saying. There was no reply.

I try to move. I want to sit up and regain my sense of position. But I feel stuck here on the floor.

"How could you waste your life, Hugo?"

Fuck. *Who* is this? The voice of a man came from the torso lying ahead of me. I tried to push back away from him. To get some distance, but my back is already curled up against the kitchen cabinets. I get a horrible chill run through my body. It runs the length of my spine, from the top of my head to my buttocks. I feel the cold sweat across my chest, under my armpits and along the length of my right chest that is touching the floor. The sensation makes me shiver.

"Hugo. Dear Hugo. Why are you chasing me for answers that you need to find out yourself?"

The voice has an accent to it. European. Deep and rugged in its nature. Worn out like the person has travelled a thousand lifetimes in one.

"Who-who are you? What do you want?" I can hear my voice quiver. I need to get up and away from this person. I need light to see what is going on. Where has she gone? She was here a few moments ago, in front of me. She was speaking to me; she was on the sofa and coming over to lie with me. Where has she gone? Who is this person and what has *he* done to her?

"Please. Please tell me what you want. Who are you?" I can feel myself panicking now. My pulse is racing. My forehead is damp with sweat and my hair is clinging to my face. My mouth is a mixture of bile and has the dryness of a concrete mixer. I can feel my tongue stick to the roof of my mouth as I try to speak and make sense of what is happening here.

I hear his breath again. There is a deep sigh, followed by a slow, controlled breath out.

"Oh, Hugo." The voice is one that I have not come across before. Not someone I recognise.

"Who are you, please? What do you want from me?"

"Stop chasing ghosts, Hugo. You are running from

your demons. Your inner pain is what is making everything tumble down around you. Look what you did to her. Look at the pain you caused."

He knows her.

"Where is she? She was here a few moments ago. What have you done to her?"

I struggle to understand the words coming out of my mouth. I feel the room spinning round and round like a rollercoaster ride now.

"You are consumed in things that you think will settle the pain within you. But you are wrong. Believe me. I know. I was you; I *am* you. I destroyed everything around me because I listened to the demons within me. Do not make my same fatal mistake."

I want to scream. I want to kick out at this person and tell him to get away. At that moment, the light shines again from above my head. It is bright and directed down into my eyes. It makes my eyes narrow as I try to adjust to the brightness.

I blink several times and focus on the figure in front of me, lying on their left side, head resting on the floor. As my vision becomes clear, I can make out this man's worn out pale face. His cheeks are drawn in and wasted. There is pain and sadness coming from within his eyes. I can make out a blue hat tight on his head. A white appendage covers the left side of his face, like an extension of his hat. It covers his right ear and tucks into his coat.

I am sure I recognise this figure. I am sure that this figure recognises me. I need to get up. I need to force myself to move.

"Even the brightest sunflowers wither away, Hugo."

I suddenly feel my heartbeat race, like it is going to

jump out of my chest.

"Vincent."

The room flashes with a bright light. My head spins and I feel I have all the air sucked out of me.

My eyes open to an empty room. The light overhead me has been switched back on, from the extractor fan. I am still on the floor. I can move and get up now. I look over to the sofa. Empty. There is no one here. I can see the empty whisky bottle lying on the floor next to me.

10

Before

I set my phone to withhold the caller ID as I reread the letter. The mobile number is at the bottom of the page, waiting for me to get in contact. My fingers hover over the digits on the phone. I have left it on purpose for a few days. Perhaps I want another letter to arrive or someone to contact me via phone first. The more I have thought it over in my mind, the more I grow suspicious that this is someone fucking with me and taking the piss out of my lack of paid work at present. It is probably that dick, Henry, from the Star freelance agency who has always laughed at my ideas of writing a detailed alternative narrative to Vincent van Gogh's mental decline. Fucking prick with his cheap suits and constant Tinder selfies. At least I had the literature-driven intellect to chase my passion. What did *he* ever have? A few freelance clients to match to jobs that paid him a commission. Big fucking deal. Twat! Actually, on second thoughts, it might not be him. The language and structure of the letter would be way beyond his shallow and narrow wavelength of words he has at his disposal. Umm, I think I am at risk of devaluing him. That's a term that I learnt from Fiona after the totally embarrassing and traumatic experience I had, first hand, of this torturous procedure that was let loose on me from someone. From someone that I held close to me. I am sorry, universe, and for my own karma; I apologise for the thoughts I have put out there about Henry. He is still a prick, however.

"Your flat white, sir." The mug is placed on the small square table as I sit at my new hang-out in darkness with the candle on the table. This place stays open until 11.00 PM, seven days a week. Its speciality is hot chocolate, made in-house, but I think I have only ever tried it once. Way too thick for me and my stomach once did flips for over a week afterwards.

"Thanks, and just tap water whenever you can." I turn my attention back to the letter. It is not busy in here this evening, good enough to call the number. I could have called from home, but I know I would have wanted to walk after the phone call, to let whatever take its time to sink in – there is nothing better than a late-night walk in London to allow that process. A process that I have done several times to maintain my own sanity. When the darkness draws in and consumes me, the walk allows me to keep some aspect of control.

The phone rings on the other end. Two rings, three, four.

"Hello Mr Jensen." Shit, they answered. The voice – a male one, deep in tone – sounded elderly.

"Huh, yes, hello. It is Hugo here, Hugo Jensen." Of course they know my name.

"Thank you for taking time to make contact. We know it must be a very strange experience for you to get a letter like the one sent. The very fact that you have waited a few days to call gives the very impression that you have made time to evaluate all aspects of this."

"Well, it's not every day a letter like that arrives. So, may I ask–" I was cut short before I could finish.

"Understandably, there will be many questions on your mind and, in fact, such questions will have grown in number as the days have progressed. Rest assured, all such questions will be answered in full and to your satisfaction. However, time is of the precious essence, as it is always, and we would like to meet, urgently."

I just stare at the candle sitting on the table. Its flame flickering. Trying to take in what has just been said to me.

"When would you like to meet and where?" I feel like going with this to see where it leads.

"Since we have you on the phone, why delay? Could you make it to a cocktail bar on 8 Broadwick Street, Soho. It's called Basement Sate."

I feel this isn't really a question for me. I also feel that if I am to pass this up tonight, right now, then either my moment will be lost, or worse, perhaps I will really piss some people off that I should not be pissing off.

"Mr Jensen, are you still there?"

"Yes, yes; sorry, yes, of course. I can make my way there now. I am not too far from that location at present."

"Excellent. When you arrive at the door, please give your name to the doorman and you will be allowed entry. Thank you again for this. It is greatly appreciated."

"Yes, sure, but–" Before I could continue, the line went dead.

I look at the phone, the empty screen showing notice that the call has ended. It is late. I am going to a meeting somewhere unfamiliar with God knows who at the other end. There are all sorts of thoughts going through my head. What if this is just a way to get me somewhere, alone, and then to hold me ransom for all my belongings? Actually, what belongings do I have that are worth taking from me? Apart from an apartment that I cannot afford the mortgage on anymore and a few clothes. I suppose I do have those few art pieces in storage, but I know they are not worth much at all. Perhaps I should call someone to accompany me or at least tell someone where I going. But the only person, perhaps, I could reach out to is Charlie and he is a good few hundred miles up north in Manchester.

The rain has started coming down with a slight drizzle. It will probably take ten minutes or so to walk from here, as long as I don't get lost. Soho's back streets are always a maze to me, sober or intoxicated, they always seem like they have changed their configuration since the last time I walked through. I know the general direction to Dean Street and Greek Street, and so if I can get there I will be able to find the location of this bar. I am sure I remember the bar's name, Basement Sate, or something like that. This is when Google comes into its own.

The street seems deserted. This does not seem like a place where a cocktail bar would be. Then again, perhaps it is the perfect place, as most bars are hidden and only the selected chosen few are aware of their locations. Like the secret elite society or the trendy crowd of Soho – the actors of screen and stage. Well, that's what they *think* they are, anyway.

"May I help you?" This greeting from a mountain of a man standing at the only doorway with a light over it in this street. I notice an earpiece in his right ear, making him look like something out of a secret service film. There is also a very distinctive scar on his face. My eyes cannot help but focus on the scar as the overhead light casts a shadow where the scar has been formed from bringing the two edges of the skin together.

"I was talking to you."

I realise I have not said a word yet. The rain is coming down in big droplets now and my hair is stuck to my forehead.

"I have been invited here this evening. I think. Is this the bar called Basement…" I try to remember the name, "…Sata?" I ask tentatively.

"You mean Basement Sate. What is your name or who has invited you, as you say?"

"My name is Hugo. Hugo Jensen. I am not sure who invited me, but they explained to give my name at the door."

The guy steps forward on hearing my name. He steps down from the doorway, to the street level with me. He still towers over me. I can feel his eyes examining me. Perhaps he has been told of my description and he is making sure it matches. Or he has been instructed to beat the crap out of me. Who knows? All I want to do is get out of the bloody rain.

As he steps aside he motions me to go through.

"Follow the steps down to the door and tell the lady that greets you that you are for table seven."

"Thanks." I walk past him and glance at a small sign on the door, 'No prostitutes work in this establishment'. The stairway is narrow and winding and I need to be sure I don't slip. I can still feel the eyes of the doorman on my back as I walk down, but I avoid looking back.

The door opens up to a dark room, lit with dim lights over the bar to the far right corner and there are tealights dotted around on tables. Music over the speakers, gently diffusing into the room with soul. I look around the room and see a handful of people scattered about. It is a youngish crowd, perhaps late 20s to mid-40s.

"Hi. Do you have a reservation?" An overly smiley and enthusiastic welcoming lady at the desk. Her right ear is full of earrings from the pinna to the helix whereas her left ear only contains one emerald stud. She is tapping her fingers on a clipboard, with a couple of tattoos on the dorsal aspect of her fingers.

"Table seven." My words come out with hesitation and a slightly suspicious tone.

I am taken to a lonely table in the corner of the room. Even my pathetic tealight is not lit.

"Drink?"

"Umm, do you do orange juice, please?"

She just smiles in response and leaves to get my drink.

Right, I suppose I just sit and wait. Minutes pass by. I sip on my orange juice, watching everyone else in here having conversations and laughing in their huddled groups. I wish I had a book or something to read. I keep the letter in my hands, not because I want it to be a sign to whoever is supposed to be meeting me, but more that it is the only thing I have to read and look like I am not a loner here. My phone battery is down to ten percent, so I need to preserve that.

"Just sticking to the hard stuff, I see." I look up at the figure standing by my side. It is the doorman from earlier. In the darkness his teeth shine like neon lights. Perhaps he got them whitened.

"I am waiting for someone so will await until they arrive to order the hard stuff."

I see his eyes focus on the letter in my hands. I fold the

letter away to take attention from it. As I do, I notice him take his jacket off and place it on the back of the chair next to me.

"This chair isn't taken, is it?" He does not wait for my reply and sits down.

His frame fills the whole chair and I worry that the legs will fold in on themselves. I can hear the wooden rivets creek as he leans closer towards me. He gestures with his massive hands for me to lean in closer also.

"We need to speak. But not here."

I can hear an accent as he speaks.

"What do you mean? I do not understand."

"The letter." He nods to the folded paper in my sweaty hands.

My eyes widen and my mouth falls open. I look between the letter and his face. Suddenly, I feel suffocated in here and can feel my back getting sweaty. He reaches across the table to me with his hand.

"My name is Femi."

I stare at his hand. I let the letter fall to the table.

"I am Hugo."

A big, gentle smile flashes across his face followed by a slight chuckle.

"I know."

He takes my hand. My hand gets lost in the big spade of a grip from him.

"We have a lot to talk about. Do not worry."

He shakes my hand up so that it forces me to look at him.

"I am here on your side. Do not worry."

11

Now

"I need to go check the boat out and make sure all is OK before you and the package come aboard."

Femi and I finally reach the location of the boat. I have been trying to block out the feeling of how tired my legs have felt in this final leg of the trek.

"Yeh, sure." I am breathless as I speak. Femi motions with his head to help unbuckle the package. At least we are now under cover of some trees here on the riverbank. It gives some much-needed shade. Femi looks around and walks back the way we have just come, to have a quick glance around. Always on guard.

"We should be OK here under cover of the bush for a while," he says reassuringly.

I open one of the bags and notice that we only have a quarter of a litre of water left. We timed it just right to get here. I offer it to Femi first. He looks at the bottle and then back at me before saying,

"It's OK. You have it. Seems like you need it more than me anyway, Hugo."

"Cheers. I was hoping you would say that." I take a couple of big swigs from the water and it feels like nectar travelling down my throat.

Femi kneels next to the package. From where I am sitting, it looks like he is speaking to a child resting on the ground. I can hear the calming whisper of the river, just beyond the bush. On the opposite bank there are great sand dunes that tower high into the sky through the trees. The slopes naturally create a shadow down them, making them inviting to roll down.

I can see the wide back of Femi as he faces away from me.

"Do you think he knew the ramifications of his work and all the pain to be caused over a hundred years after they were painted?"

It was not like Femi to get so inquisitive about the package. He must be getting soft with the exhaustion.

"I think, at the time, it was his way of expressing his inner emotions with the world around him. Something deep inside me makes me think that he knew the messages would stay around long after he was gone." I say this as I can relate directly to van Gogh's struggle. Femi did not respond. He just stayed kneeling at the package.

"Femi? You OK?" I could see his back rise and fall as he took deep breaths in and out.

I thought it was best just to let him be with his thoughts. I always hate it when people ask if I'm OK as I keep myself to myself. Or when I might be forced to go and mingle with others to take my mind off things. Maybe I just want to be in my own company and not be around others. Perhaps the others were the problem. Why is it so difficult for people to just let others be alone and deal with their inner voice?

"Do you miss home?"

"Sorry, what was that?" He spun around on the spot

and sat down on the grass. There is a breeze now coming to hit my face. I can see the grass and the bushes moving in unison with the direction of the wind. Although it is a warm breeze, it is still a welcome reprieve from the humid heat sticking to every inch of my skin.

Femi picks at a blade of grass.

"Home. Tell me about your home, Hugo. London."

As Femi moves the blade of grass through his fingers, I see the sadness in his posture now. Can this poor fool also be as broken as me inside?

"I was born and raised in London. All I know is London." I stop. I know what I *really* want to say, but I also know that I find it immensely difficult to talk about the real emotion I have with London.

"It's a great city. I almost feel as though London is mine and everyone else in it are just visitors." I try to get Femi to come out of whatever darkness he is in. "I guess I should charge rent for everyone who is in *my* London." I give a fake laugh, but Femi does not bite.

"You seemed so alone, Hugo. I mean, in London. You just seemed to be lost and yet you say it is your home."

I look away from him. He is making me feel uncomfortable. I look back to the towering dunes on the opposite bank. I think to myself how beautiful the contrast of dry sand and rich, green leaves and trees are in this land.

"I'm sorry, Hugo. I should not be concerned so much in aspects like that. It is not my place to ask such things."

I sigh. Maybe he just cares. Maybe he wants to be a friend. Like, a real genuine friend.

"No. No need to say sorry, Femi. It's just…" I clench my jaw, "…it's just complicated, that's all."

There is a moment where we just sit and look at each other. Like we both understand that there is more to this conversation than is being played out. There is more said in that silence than in the spoken word between us.

"You going to be OK here for a bit, alone?"

"What do you mean?" Fuck, is he leaving me?

"I mean, just for a few moments. I need to go down to the river. My cousin's boat should be waiting just up the shore over that mount. I am sure we are safe here."

Of course. He just wants to make sure we are safe, that's all. He is not abandoning me.

"Yeh. I will stay here and keep guard of the package."

Femi gets up, pads down his pants and feels for the protein bar he put in his cargo pockets on our earlier stop. He gets it out and snaps it in half, wrapper and all. He throws one half over to me.

"Here. Share this with me. I will be back in a bit. Just scream if anything you feel isn't right."

Before I can say anything, while I pick up the half bar of protein that landed at my feet, I see the back of Femi striding away through the reeds. A few migrating birds fly out of cover into the sky as Femi darts off.

I let the sounds get my attention now. Trying to take in all the beauty of what this place is. I really have not had any time to appreciate the wonder of this country since we arrived. Trying to stay alive and keep on the move has been all-consuming. Had I known it would be this way, I would probably never have called the number on that letter, back in London. What did I have as an alternative? My life in London, as Femi put it. What is waiting for me in London now? If I were to stay here, to perish away with no food or water, to let the heat burn through my skin and to leave nothing but my bones to rest on the grass here, to be eventually covered with sand, who would mourn for me? Who in London would cry out and question 'where is Hugo Jensen?' Perhaps the bank chasing up mortgage repayments. But apart from them.

Glancing at my cheap imitation military watch, it's been about five minutes since Femi left. Let's see, perhaps five to ten minutes getting down to the shore and locating the boat. Then a few minutes more to ensure it is safe before approaching it. I assume his cousin has not seen him for a while. What did he say his name was – Kunlee? So, perhaps a ten-minute catch-up. 'Blah-blah-blah, how have you been? You look good; how's the family, the business? Blah-blah-blah'. Then I assume Femi would want to ensure that the boat is safe and that no unwanted visitors are hiding on or below the decks. So, he may ask for a tour. Then, when Femi is finally satisfied, he would say that he is coming back to get me. So, all in all, perhaps 30 minutes until Femi returns. That sounds logical in my head. Unless it all goes south and something goes wrong.

The heat really makes me want to sleep. Obviously, that is out of the question as I am on duty to protect the package. Why is it always at times when I need to stay awake that I feel I could so easily fall asleep? Why can this feeling not be present when normal people sleep, at night, at a decent time when the night sky is dark outside?

Pacing around will keep my mind focused. The package catches my eye. I still cannot believe that it is here, in my presence. Just lying there, on the ground. I mean, what a mindfuck. I am in Egypt, with one of the most powerful discoveries of all time, here at my feet – literally. How do you get your head around that? Wait until I discuss this all with Fiona. Damn! Fiona. What day is it? I didn't let her know that I would not be present for my therapy sessions. She will worry about me if I do not show up or make contact by phone or e-mail. I will have to ask Femi if there is a way I can make contact. As Fiona said, I was one of the more vulnerable clients because of the state of my mind and the aspects as my unconscious memory is allowing my conscious mind to remember all the true holes that I blacked out. I hope she does not worry too much about me. Crap, there I go again, worrying about others rather than me.

I will check the closure aspects of the package again to make sure it's safe and kill some time. The grass is so dry close up. I hope there are not any scorpions lurking around. I am sure I read that they are rife around Egypt, as they can survive with little water. Knowing my luck, I will get bitten by one and suffer an agonisingly slow, painful death by the time Femi returns. Gosh, shake that from my mind. Positive manifestations, not anything dark and sinister.

Ummm, I am tempted so much to have a peek at the package. A little look, just to make sure it is OK. I am sure that will be OK. Why should I not be allowed? Just unzip one of the edges and let my eyes settle on the beauty of the package that rests safely within the casing. Femi would not be angry if I just took a few seconds to ensure it was safe. In fact, I would be doing him a favour, to reassure him that we have done well and kept it safe. For his boss. Whoever that may be. He assured me that I would meet his boss once we get to Cairo for the safe handover of the package. That would perhaps be the only time that I actually get to be up close and personal with it. To have my own intimate time with it. That is why I was brought along on this trip.

To be sure it is the real thing. To study it. To appraise it. To give my intellect on the authenticity of it. But, bloody hell! Why do they trust me with such a task? I mean, there are so many others worldwide, with experience, with credentials that can fill a suitcase. Those who come with international recommendation, rather than me. Someone who has no real background in such work, apart from my obsessive research into Vincent. The research that I have compiled over years. Perhaps that is the very reason I have been chosen for this. The undiluted nature of my work. Just a little peek now won't hurt anyone. Femi does not need to know.

"Hugo."

Fuck, why did I not hear Femi returning? He is like an overgrown master Yoda in stealth mode. I freeze where I am. On my knees, hands on the side zip of the package, ready to unzip one end to have a look at the contents.

I spin around and see Femi standing tall with his hands resting on his hips. Tall and strong, as ever.

"You are back. H-how did it go?" He knows what I was doing. My voice gives it away. His eyes move from my face to the package behind me and then back to me.

"Yes, Hugo. All is set. The boat is secure and my cousin is there. He is waiting for us."

I can tell from Femi's voice that he is not impressed with me.

"I was just—"

"I know; it has its own pull. I know it speaks to you, Hugo. But you know the deal. We need to keep it protected at all times."

I hear the words from Femi and I know them all too well. It was me – yes, me – that explained the importance of keeping the heat and humidity away from the surface of the package in this terrain, hence the need for the outer casing.

I feel my face burn with embarrassment.

"I was just checking the zips were tight and secure."

Fuck. I know I have let him down.

12

Before

I feel like a train has hit me, over and over again and then run me over, over and over again. My eyes ache and so badly I want to close and rest them, but my sleep is worse than ever now. The bloody mirror never lies. I really can't face looking at myself. Not just because of the state of my tired worn skin but also, looking into my eyes, I can see deep into me. Into the troubled dark thoughts that lay hidden in the depths. Crap, did I really drink all that whisky, alone, again last night? The bottle resting on the dining table and the stained glass sitting beside it. Fiona would absolutely be disappointed in me. She always says how impressed she is with how much progress I am making. But using any substance to repress mood and emotion is never a good thing.

Man, my stomach is a mixture of acid and bile. I can't face any food at present. Coffee and water are all that I crave. That and a cocktail of aspirin and Gaviscon. I can hear my phone. Where is it? The sound is coming from the sofa. It's tucked away behind a cushion. Damn, it's already 10.45 AM. Private number flashes up on the screen. Probably one of those junk calls. Last thing I need this morning.

"Yes, hello," I answer.

"Hugo. Why haven't you been picking up the phone? I have been calling since 8.00 AM."

The voice on the other end sounds vaguely familiar. Still struggling to focus, my head feels like it is in a vice.

"Hugo!"

"Yes, yes; I am here. Sorry, who is this?"

I hear a deep sigh on the other end of the phone.

"Femi." Silence on the other end.

"I am so sorry. I didn't realise the time. I, I didn't—"

He cut me off.

"You got drunk and passed out last night, right? And you just woke up now."

I was not sure what I could say to that. It was a very accurate assessment of the events.

"Look. Get in the shower, go throw up or whatever, have coffee and get down to the coffee shop where we said we would meet."

I heard the words, but was having slight difficulty in registering them fully.

"Meet me in Covent Garden. Just come to the station and I will be outside. Then we can go together, get that coffee and speak like we should have done over an hour ago."

The phone goes dead.

I sheepishly step onto the street from the exit of the station. It's busy as it's now approaching lunchtime. Femi is easy to spot. He is leaning on the wall across the street as I come out of the ticket turnstiles. He does not look impressed at all. I can tell that his normal relaxed face is tense.

"Sorry, Femi."

"Let's go down to Neal's Yard, it's round the corner and we can sit in private outside." He led the way and I followed with my tail between my legs.

"You look like shit. What happened?" We sat at a table outside in the small courtyard. Femi had his black Americano and I had my flat white sitting on the table.

"Trouble sleeping again, unfortunately, and so I started off with just one drink, which obviously just morphed into a few back-to-back drinks." I couldn't look at Femi in the eyes as I spoke. Over the last couple of weeks, he has taken me under his wing on several aspects, bringing me up to speed on the background as to who and why that letter was delivered to me.

"How many times have I told you? Do not ever drink alone at home. You should call me if you ever get that way." This is why I feel like I have let him down. It's only been two weeks or so since Femi introduced himself to me, but we have met every day and spoken constantly. Not just related to the work we need to do, but I feel he has become a friend – a *real* friend.

"I know. I feel so bad not only letting myself down, but you also." I still avoid eye contact.

"Look, Hugo. This isn't about letting anyone down. I recognise trauma in someone. And you, my friend, have an abundance of it. But it is not my job to get you to talk and open up. But it *is* my job to keep you focused and safe. And that means away from shit like you did last night."

I get the strength to look at him now.

"Understood." He wants evidence that I have taken it in.

"Yes, Femi. Understood," I reiterate.

"Right, now we have that sorted, let's get down to what

we have to discuss." He takes a sip of his hot drink. He seems much calmer now compared to when we met at the station.

"Femi. Before we get to that…. May I ask a few things that have been on my mind?"

From the expression on his face, I feel that he knew these questions were coming. I mean, up till now, I have trusted everything he has said and gone by his lead. He has reassured me that I am safe. He has explained how I am being recruited as a consultant concerning advising on rare artefacts in relation to Vincent van Gogh. He has explained that his employer is a very influential family interested in Vincent. How I came to their attention when they spotted my online article entitled 'The not so lost world of Van Gogh'. I explained why I feel some of his paintings are hidden around the world. And my reasons were backed up by years of painstaking research. But what followed was a number of comments under the article ridiculing what I had written. Emojis of laughing faces and tears coming down them. But Femi explained that, after reading my article, along with the comments giving them entertainment, the family now wanted my expertise to validate a certain artefact that they may or may not have in their possession as yet. All very cloak-and-dagger, but I was getting paid for my time and work. Money that I so badly needed.

But what was *not* clear to me and what I had not questioned as yet was how Femi came to work for such a family. So I asked him.

"How did you come to work for the family? I mean, it's not your run-of-the-mill job, is it? I mean, you are like a secret agent of some sort." I can tell my effort at being inquisitive was perhaps not what Femi had time for today. But if I am beginning to trust this guy, I need to know more.

Femi leans back in his chair. He spreads his legs out in front of him and crosses them at the ankles. He takes his warm drink in his hands and lets out a sigh before taking a sip.

"It's a long story, but I suppose giving you the short answer would give you an indication of my intentions and, more importantly, give you the confidence that you can trust me. I hope." As he speaks, I can recognise that he, too, perhaps has been through some aspect of hardship and still carries those burdens with him. People with torment and pain end up realising such pain in others' eyes.

"I was working as a porter in a hotel in the main tourist district of Zimbabwe a few summers ago. It was basic work, welcoming guests as they arrived. Ensuring their luggage was safely taken to their rooms and so on. The work was straightforward, but the hours were long. Often 16-hour days to cover the lack of staff."

Femi's voice is much softer than I have heard in the past weeks.

"On one such uneventful day, in the late afternoon, there arrives an elderly gentleman. Very quintessentially dressed. He made an impression straight away. Not many people can pull off having a white flower pinned to their jacket lapel and having a long tail coat on in the heat. But he did it with style."

I realise that the guy Femi describes sounds very similar in description to the guy I came across in the National Gallery that day. I don't interrupt Femi and let him continue.

"So, I got to settle this guy in. Make sure his luggage was accounted for and see if his room was to his expectations. He seemed as though he did not want anyone to make a fuss over him. Over the following few days, he did not venture out of the hotel complex. He would wander from his room to the various reading lounges around the hotel. I don't even think I recall him using any other facilities such as the spa or health fitness centre. He would just sit and read."

The courtyard around us is now filling up with people for lunch. But we are both still pretty much secluded from the others and our conversation remains between us. I liked this softer side to Femi in contrast to the fake, hard-nosed doorman he had been trying to play.

"I got to come across that guy several times while I was going about my jobs in the hotel," Femi continued. "Then, one morning, just after breakfast, I was waxing some of the visitors' cars out the back. He approached me to ask why I was always at work for what seemed to be every hour of the day and night."

There was a pause from Femi. He looked away from me as if in deep thought.

"Well, anyway, long story short, he was impressed by my work ethic and asked if I was committed to staying working at the hotel and, indeed, committed to being tied down to the continent of Africa."

"And I suppose your answer to both of those questions was a no, hence you now work for this man."

There was a nod in agreement from him as he reached for his drink. It was obvious from his facial expression that there was much more to the choice than he wanted to tell me at this stage. I did not have the respect as yet to push him. But it troubled me that a man of his age could leave his country just like that. Was he leaving or was he running from something?

"This guy... So, he is the one that wrote the letter to me."

"Perhaps, or someone in the same family. I do not know much of the dynamics, but the family is vast and spread all over the world. Very much an elitist type of structure."

I am curious to know if this guy is here in London.

"So, have you done many of these missions for the family? Or am I the first like this?"

Femi just smiled back at me and then leant forward into the table.

"Don't you trust me, Hugo?"

"Hey. This is coming from the guy who pretended to be a doorman."

"OK, but in fairness, I had to be sure it was you and that you came alone. Not because you are in danger." Femi saw the change in my facial expression at his words, so he retracted. "As in the nature of the work is sensitive and so, just wanting to get the appropriate steps in place. That's all."

I can feel my head pounding again. I should have brought some paracetamol along with me. How the hell am I supposed to concentrate with a hangover?

"OK. So, what's next? You have spent the last few days looking over all the research and information I have gathered and put together over the years regarding Vincent van Gogh. No doubt you have been reporting back. So, what is it that they actually want me to do?"

Femi pulled out a small notebook from his inner breast pocket with a pencil. He opened it up to the middle pages and drew something on it. At first, I thought he was drawing a child's face with a stick body. But as he continued and then spun it around to show me it was clear that it was a collection of sunflowers he had drawn.

I reached across the table to take the notebook, but Femi did not take his hands off it, just stared at me and shook his head. He ripped the page out of the book and tore the paper into tiny pieces.

Sunflowers. This was all about the *Sunflowers*. Damn. So, what I always suspected is actually true. Fuck! This is massive. And fuck, my head hurts.

13

Now

I followed Femi in silence as we travelled over the ridge and towards the riverbank. I knew he was disappointed at the fact that I had been close to perhaps opening the casing and having a look at the package. It was best not to say anything when Femi was in this mood. He had this way about him where he could say a million words by saying nothing at all. Femi was carrying the package on his back for this final leg. As we got closer to the river, the green rich colour of the leaves and trees got more intense. They seemed so full of life and made you just want to hold them and suck all the nutritional aspects from them. I could see, down in the distance, a boat resting by the bank. It was green also, with blue aspects to the deck. At a distance it looked solid and confident as a vessel. But as I got closer and was able to focus on the boat, it looked worn and as if it had witnessed many years of life at sea. The hum of the engine was filling the air around it. I could just make out a few people on the deck – three bodies, just moving around, pulling this and putting that over there. They all wore caps to shield their eyes from the sun.

Then I spotted who would have been Femi's cousin. He was standing on shore peeling a banana and I could see his big white teeth reflecting in the sun. The teeth must run in the family.

"You OK back there?" Femi shouted.

"Yep! All good! That's an impressive boat!" I shouted back. As soon as I heard myself, I thought, *"What a dick!"* Of course it's not an impressive boat. But it was the only thing I could think of.

"You must not have seen many boats. It's a shit-hole, but it will serve its purpose and get us where we need to go." I am sure I heard a slight chuckle in Femi's voice.

"This must be your pale brother from London." The joyful voice came out loud and confident from Kunlee, as he wrestled with a mouthful of banana.

"Hugo, meet Kunlee, my useless cousin on my mother's side."

I was carrying the two bags, one in each hand. As I approached Kunlee, he held out a hand to me. His hand looked strong, but weathered. Cracked skin all over his fingers and nails that had all manner of dirt caught under them.

"Mr Hugo. Welcome to the Nile." I was not sure how to reach for his hand, but he took a bag from my right hand and turned to lead the way onto the boat. I followed him while Femi came up behind me. I could see the smooth head of Kunlee from the back. He was taller than me, but not as tall as Femi. He walked with a slight forward tilt to his hip, like he could not straighten up fully. He was wearing a sweat-stained blue checked shirt that was only half-buttoned.

"Thank you, Kunlee. It certainly has been a flash tour so far."

"Come, come. You should take the weight off you and

settle in while we make final checks before we head off. Zeno! Zeno, where are you? Come here now."

Kunlee looked around his vessel with an immense proud feeling.

"The ship crew is small and lazy! Zeno, come on now."

Then, from the corner of my vision, a small figure wearing a cap came scuttering towards us as we stood on deck.

"Yes, sir, I was just making sure—" His voice seemed unsure of himself and Kunlee cut him off.

"Yes, yes. Never mind that now. I want you to take our guests below deck to their rooms. Take their bags and ensure they settle in well."

Zeno took the bag from Kunlee and also reached for the bag I was holding.

"No, it's OK; I got this," I said as I smiled at him.

We were led below deck to a small area that was our room to share. It was dark, but cooler than up on deck. The engine's hum was louder down here and I could feel its vibrations under my feet. Zeno left without saying a word after settling my bag down.

"We will be safe here. We can trust Kunlee," Femi said once he closed the door behind Zeno. He turned away from me, motioning for me to start the procedure to get the package off his back.

"What does he know? I mean, is there anything I need to know about what you have told him about our..." I paused. I was not quite sure what to call this. Our mission, our job, our research, our prize or our loot?

Once we got the package onto the bed Femi sat down on the corner chair to unbuckle his boots.

"He knows we are meeting some art dealers in Cairo

and need transport up the Nile. As far as he is concerned, you work as an art appraiser and are here to appraise some pieces in Cairo."

"Do not worry," Femi continued, seemingly sensing my hesitation. He looked up at me from the chair. "My cousin has no sense of art and so I will be surprised if he asks anything at all. He likes speaking about himself in any case, so we will be hearing a lot of stories about him, most likely."

It was nice to get a change of clothes. There was a small sink in the room and a tight shower cubicle next to our room. Being conscious of the need to save some of the clean water while we were stationary, I used the sink and a towel to just wipe the dirt and sweat from my tired body and put on another t-shirt and some shorts. I left my big boots to air just outside our door and decided to walk around bare foot on the deck. Femi took his time unpacking some of the contents from his bag and placing them on the shelf above the bed.

I could now feel the boat moving, making its way up the Nile to Cairo. The engine sound grew louder and there were other sounds now evident, with clangs of chains and voices of the crew shouting and receiving orders. It was hard to make out what exactly was being said.

"Let's go have some supper with my cousin on deck and then we can get some much-needed rest." Femi was as exhausted as me, it seemed.

It was about 700 kilometres to Cairo, give or take, and the boat would go all night and we would arrive in the morning without stopping.

"Meet you up top," Femi said as he left the room before me.

The boat's movement took me back to when I wanted to plan a cruise with her. I had always wanted to see the Northern Lights and thought having a cruise around that part of the world would be something that we would both enjoy. I never got to suggest it to her, but it always burns away at me. If only I had perhaps made more of an effort to show how much I actually enjoyed spending time around her, things would have turned out differently. As I had explored with Fiona, when I felt things were going so well with her, when I actually felt myself happy around her, I felt out of my normal comfort zone. My version of normal that I was programmed to be, according to Fiona, was that I was always in that 'flight or fight mode'. So, for me, if I felt happiness or of feeling comfortable, it was an alien emotion. My unconscious mind wanted me to feel anxiety, guilt, fear and pain. Thus, a simple suggestion of spending time on a cruise with her to see the Northern Lights, became an act of anxiety and fear. Hence, it never occurred. Oh well, things to work on, I guess.

I had not realised how late in the day it had become. I am sure the sun was high up in the sky just a few moments ago when we boarded the boat. As I walk up onto the deck, I can see how dark the day has got. I have left my amazing watch back in the room. I can hear the voices of Femi and his cousin coming from the far end of the boat, so I wander in their direction.

"London man. Come, come." The joyful voice of Kunlee resonates across the deck to me. He moves a chair closer to the makeshift table, a collection of wooden crates.

"Zeno! Bring the food. We will eat now."

I glance over at Femi as I take a seat opposite him. He smiles at me and I can see how gentle he seems now.

This gives me comfort that all is OK and we are safe on this boat.

"So, my cousin tells me you do things with paintings." Kunlee looks over to me while he leans back in his chair, legs spread out in front of him.

"Well, I don't really do any paintings myself. I just know a lot of boring facts about paintings and so people ask me for my advice of certain things regarding that."

Femi was right. As soon as I said that, I can tell that Kunlee is switching off. To my surprise, he asks me more.

"What got you into such work with paintings?"

This is a question that makes me think. I can sense Femi lean forward from his seat towards me, anticipating my answer also.

"Well, it goes back to my school days." Zeno arrives with a jug full of water and glasses. I am thirsty but will wait for Femi to give me the all clear to have the water as we have stuck to bottled water until now.

"I always enjoyed art as a subject at school. Not only for the creative side, but also the history of paintings and the artists that painted them at the time."

Femi leans forward again to pick up the jug of water to fill the three glasses.

"Ah, so you are a romantic historian at heart, hey." Kunlee follows his statement with a deep laugh.

"Well, art is a form of expressionism. It reflects what the person was feeling and thinking when they created that particular piece. It is a personal story and message from the person to the world. One could say that the artist is showing their innermost emotions for us to criticise."

"Tell me, Hugo." Femi's voice makes me turn my head towards him. I can see how genuinely invested he is in what I am saying. "What is the one piece of art that either you have done yourself or of another artist, that stands out from all the others?"

This is interesting from Femi. It is actually reminiscent of a therapy type of question. I did not have to think too hard to answer.

"It is *The Starry Night* by Vincent van Gogh."

"Ah. I have heard of this painting." Kunlee disrupts the intimacy between Femi and I. He continues. "It is the one when the artist went mad, correct?"

I ignore the comment from Kunlee. So does Femi.

"Why that one? What is it about that painting, Hugo?" Femi pushes for more.

"I remember being captivated by his complex arrangement of colours and strokes of the brush close up, yet, at a distance, it creates the perfect landscape. It draws you in to wonder how the artist felt at that moment. What he was going through and what message he wanted to deliver to us all as we studied the painting."

I let the words hang there. I could see Kunlee being distracted by everything around him. He was not interested in this conversation.

"Did you study it at school then?" Femi asks.

"I actually chose to draw it with pastels when I was aged around 12." I can tell my voice is becoming softer and my throat tightens slightly. "It took me ten days to get it exactly how I wanted it to look. It was for an art display at school."

I look away from Femi, over to the evening sky making its way around us. I can see a migration of birds in the distance, following the river's bend.

"Were you happy with the final finished version?" Femi

brings my concentration back to the conversation. Like he sensed I was hesitant to continue.

I take a deep breath in. My blink is slow and deliberate. I need to be careful how I answer this, so it does not set me of.

"It was perfect. Just perfect."

Femi and I lock eyes for a second before he leans back in his chair and folds his arms across his chest and smiles.

"Perfect," he repeats.

"Let's eat!" Kunlee shouts and brings us all back to now.

As Femi and I walk back to our room after dinner, we take in the night unfolding around us at the river. The dark navy blackness replaces the richness of the green bushes and trees.

"What happened to *The Starry Night* painting you did as a child?" Femi asks while opening our door.

I stand behind him having wished he would not ask that question, yet I know that he was saving it for when we were alone.

"I lost it. At school."

Femi paused, his back to me with his hand on the door about to walk through.

"That's a shame."

I knew he did not believe my answer. But how do you explain that someone who was supposed to care for me and show me love and keep me safe destroyed something that was so perfect and something that I was so proud of? But instead, I got punished for being creative and doing something that I was happy doing. Can't choose our parents, hey.

14

Before

The week would take so long to come around. It seemed as though Thursdays kept getting further and further away from the previous Thursday. I was hesitant to ask Fiona to increase sessions to more than once a week, for two main reasons: 1) I really could not afford much more than I was already having cost-wise, and 2) I knew I would perhaps have an issue coming out of the co-dependency I was having with Fiona. Although this was a safe space for me, I was still yet to understand how to take what I had learnt in the sessions out into the real world on the outside.

This Thursday was different. I also had Femi to deal with. It felt strange that I had to keep my therapy sessions from him. I felt strange in the comfort that I had Femi around me already. Could it be that I was actually gaining a friend that wanted to be a real person to me? I had no choice but to trust him with how this situation was unfolding, but on the same level, how would I have come across such a person if it was not at all related to my work and research that I had done? But I wanted to believe that I could attract people as friends. Perhaps this was something I needed to discuss in my session today. Obviously without mentioning any names or the circumstances around how

Femi and I have come into contact.

> 'Hope you are up and sober. We have to get some
> work done today to make arrangements for when
> we travel. What are your movements today?'

The text message came through from Femi midmorning. I felt that he knew somehow that perhaps I would have still been lying in bed, staring at the ceiling if the message was sent any earlier. I should have been feeling guilty for being in bed so late as I had been made aware that my time was being paid for daily, hourly and even minute by minute. Femi was very direct with this when we first discussed the arrangements and also his 'boss' had arranged an upfront payment before I had even agreed, to be transferred to my bank account. Was this a bribe or was it a means for me not to be able to say no?

I roll over to my side to face the window. I can see the rays of light breaking through the ceiling to floor blinds. I hate that sensation of the day getting on with its routine outside while I wallow around in self-pity indoors.

I need to shower and try and invent some form of breakfast from the contents of my fridge and get certain things ready for Femi. We had decided it was imperative that all the thousands of words I had written or collected over time about Vincent van Gogh needed some form of order to them. Even I was now embarrassed at the disorganised chaos of my paperwork on the subject. If I got a sense of dread when thinking about all the mess of my paperwork, how the hell could I present such research to others? Femi was clear that the main aspect he, or his boss needed, was the work and discovery in relation to the

Sunflowers collection. That was a relief to me, as those were aspects I had concentrated on at one point in time and so they should all be filed together somewhere.

> 'I have been getting everything in order since morning. Only just seen this message. Shall we meet around, say, 3.30 PM?'

I sent the message back to Femi, obviously a lie about working all morning on this. I knew he would also pick this up. I have my therapy session at 2.00 PM and really do not fancy explaining this to Femi.

I can see the typing bubble on the screen of the phone. Femi forming his response.

'3.30 PM, that is all the day gone, but sure, if you need that much time, sure. Location to meet later.'

Fuck, Femi knows I am stalling for time. At least he messaged and didn't call to speak with me.

> 'How about meet outside Bond Street station and we can walk over to a coffee place?'
> 'OK. See you later.'

I lay the phone back on the empty pillow beside me. Forget breakfast, I will only have time to shower, rummage through the collection of notebooks I have on my research and then get my butt into town near Fiona's office. I will get something close by there, a sandwich or something.

"You seem more distracted than normal today, Hugo." Fiona was quick to sense something new and different about me. Was I that transparent or was Fiona that good at reading my body language and emotions? I was hoping it would be the latter as, if it were the former, it would really freak me out that everyone out there could see right through my masks.

I shift on the sofa, as always, before trying to formulate my answer.

"Just a new project with work is playing on my mind, that's all."

She smiles back in response.

"That's exciting, I trust. Work, I mean. An exciting project."

"Well, it's early days yet, but potentially it is something that really is right up my street with art."

I can see Fiona taking a long, thoughtful pause. She is well aware that I can get lost in respect of my passion for art and history and, at times, use it as a distraction to what is really going on with my life.

"Am I allowed to ask what the project is?"

"Well, it's along what we touched on last time. It focuses on Vincent van Gogh and some of his paintings. Well, in particular, the *Sunflowers* series of paintings."

Femi comes to mind now. I am sure that I am not breaching any aspect of the terms of work with him by discussing this with Fiona. I mean, I am not saying anything that is totally confidential here. Or am I?

"What is your favourite painting by him?"

Phew, Fiona has moved on from the particulars of the project anyway. That puts me at ease, although the answer to her question may form some basis of today's session. It is like she manufactured this question all along and knew we would get to this point somehow. How does she do that?

"They all are amazing. They reflect so many different variations of him and the time he was going through. But if I was to choose…" I pause. I remind myself that I am in a safe space here. I cannot help but look away from Fiona.

"Where has that taken you, Hugo?"

There it is, right on cue.

I take a deep breath. Force myself to look at her.

"Back to school. I must have been around 12 years of age or perhaps slightly younger. Sorry, dates and times are still very fuzzy for me." She nods her head in reassurance that's it's OK not to remember every detail.

"I did a drawing of *The Starry Night* by Vincent. You know, the one with the night sky over the monastery of Saint-Paul-de-Mausole."

"Yes, yes. That's a beautiful piece."

"That painting is so beautiful, but yet so misunderstood by everyone." I can see that gets Fiona thinking again.

"How do you mean?"

"Well, Vincent always painted what he saw. However, this painting did not resemble anything of what he saw from the lunatic asylum he was admitted at the time. The misconception is that this was the view from his room. But it bears no resemblance at all."

"Well…" Fiona puts her legs up on the sofa chair, sits on them and says, "…I never knew that."

"The whole painting has this dream-like emotion to it."

"So, Hugo, why does this particular painting and memory of your childhood stand out?"

She never gives up.

I feel I want the sofa to open and swallow me into the cushions. It is just recently that some of the dark blanks of memory are starting to resurface. This is one of those memories. I glance over to my left and see the clock resting on the window ledge. I know that at 2.50 PM on the dot,

Fiona will say, 'That's where we need to leave it for today'. I need to plan what I say to ensure that I am fit to see Femi afterwards. I know how sometimes I can feel rather devoid of emotion and energy after a session.

"I loved painting. It made me concentrate and forget on everything around me. Made me forget all that was going on in my life at the time. I always put my all into it. No matter what." I can feel my voice getting softer now, in a way that I hope my words leave the room without being registered.

"This painting took me around ten days to finish. I used pastels as my medium. I remember using my break times and lunch hours to sit in the art room and continue with it throughout that week. It became, I suppose, my safe place at that time."

Flashes of the days flood back. I can remember the dullness to the days outside, as it was autumn time when I did the painting. A girl called Esin would also spend time there, with me, finishing her work. It became like our special club.

"It's strange because I don't think I can remember anything else apart from that painting and those days in that art room from that time of my life."

"That's very normal when it comes to a traumatic event of some sort, especially in childhood. The memory tends to keep certain events locked away," Fiona says as I continue to avoid direct eye contact with her.

"Well, I eventually finished it and I was very proud of myself for the dedication to getting it exactly how I had wanted it. My art teacher at the time was also very impressed. But again, I am having difficulty putting a face or a name to that teacher."

My shoulders start to tighten up and I can feel how uncomfortable I am within my own body leading up to speaking out about this. Again, I naturally rub my neck and reach for my necklace when I start to feel fearful.

"Go on, Hugo…"

I swallow the dry saliva down my throat.

"The piece was displayed in the school art show and got several amazing reviews and comments. Then, once the show was over…" Here it comes. I need to hold it together. I must see Femi soon.

"…I took the painting home. My pride and joy. Something that I took time creating reflected my passion, inner emotion and character and the true me as a child. What was on that canvas was a mirror of the child in me. I don't think I have ever been so proud of my own achievements since that moment."

"What happened when you took the painting home?"

Suddenly, darkness comes over me. I feel so small sitting here now. Sitting in this room. I feel the walls moving in closer and the air being sucked out, leaving me to suffocate.

"He… he was not impressed. He felt it was not a subject that added to his perception of what he wanted me to be. He felt I had let him down. It was not a worthy skill or passion to have in art or of being creative."

Fiona leans forward to try to meet my gaze and softly prompts me to acknowledge it.

"Say who he is. Do not let the mind create the dark box."

"My father. My father tore it to shreds in front of me. I remember standing there in the hallway, just by the stairs as I got in from school. He was home from night shift at work, so he just got up. I remember him standing there with a half-sleeve button shirt on, tucked into his trousers, with a white vest showing underneath. His belt, brown with a shiny brass buckle around his waist, just waiting to do its work for him."

I can feel my eyes burn. They are narrowing due to the burn and the tears that are bursting to come through. I need to hold it together. There is a strategically placed box of tissues already beside me.

I take my time to compose my voice again.

"I watched the pieces of paper fall to the floor there in the hallway, in slow motion. It appeared time had slowed right down at that moment. I was unsure if I was to pick up the pieces and clean the mess or apologise for letting him down. But, the choice was taken away from me in that moment. I heard the buckle loosen and the familiar rap of the belt being pulled out through the trousers."

I stop talking. I don't want to speak the words out anymore. But I know I need to. I know Fiona will be gentle with me, but will want me to say it. To speak it out loud instead of being locked away.

"Hugo. Please, go on."

"He was always so clever as not to leave many marks, if any. Always in areas where it would be difficult for anyone to notice." I try and concentrate on meeting Femi soon. We will discuss the work on the research I have done and how impressed he will be when I tell him of my discoveries.

"He liked to…." I stall with my words, "…he liked to combine things. Like on this occasion. He tightened the belt around my legs so tight that I could see my feet go pale and numb. At the same time, he made me…" I panic, look at the clock, hope it is 2.50 so that our time is up. I can feel myself trembling now. "He made me do things to him with my mouth."

I sit there. The room is now in silence. I cannot look at Fiona. I just want to get up and leave the room without another word. The shame and guilt festers within me. In my mind, I see the torn pieces of my ten-day daydream lying there, on the floor, scattered everywhere, just like my child mind had become.

15

Now

I can't see his face. There is a dark hole where the features of the face should be. The hooded figure stands over me. I can tell his eyes are looking right at me, even though there are no facial features to see – just darkness where his face should be. I can just make out the shoulders and arms, resting by his side. Not moving at all. Just leaning over slightly from the waist. He stands there. Watching. The room is dark around him, yet he stands out amongst the black canvas like a halo. I want to scream, but feel totally paralysed. I am sure he is not touching me, but I feel weighted down with intense weight pressing down on my shoulders. Pushing me deeper into the bed. Fuck, I can't move. My breathing becomes laboured and I can feel the tightness in my chest. Constricting like a tight metal vice, being screwed to the maximum compression, gradually, with intent to make me feel every aspect of the pain of anticipation.

This figure looks on, standing there. My back is soaked in sweat, giving the bed sheets an extensive damp puddle beneath my torso. Maybe I can use my legs to kick him. Throw him off balance and then roll over to my right side, out the bed on the other side and form my escape. Damn.

It's no use; he must have tied my legs together at my ankles and across my thighs, as I cannot move either of my legs. Fuck, what if he has drugged me? I don't remember drinking or eating anything earlier that tasted off. But perhaps he came in and injected me while I was sleeping and then waited for the toxins to kick in. Fuck, that's it. Must be a snake toxin that causes paralysis. I remember seeing a documentary on Netflix about various gangs in New York that started using snake toxins in needles to paralyse young people in the club scene. Fuck, that is it – that is what has occurred to me.

I can feel my mouth open, but why are no words coming out? I am struggling to get any sound out at all. I can see movement just to the side of this figure. My eyes move towards the movement, but my head feels bolted down to the bed. It is like a head bracket is buckled to my forehead and then drilled down, either side of my neck, deep into the bed. I will, with all my might, lift my head off the pillow and look to the side of this figure to see the area of movement. But it is fucking useless. Not even a millimetre of movement. All I can feel is the cold, uncomfortable dampness of my sweat all over the back of my neck. I feel the hairs on it stand to attention as I feel something, a gentle, unnerving touch on my leg. Just above my left ankle. For the first time, I am aware that all I am wearing is my boxers and nothing else. The touch is gentle and slow. From what I can tell, and the movement that fits from the side of this figure, it is his hand. Yet the rest of his torso remains still, fixed in its statue there, slightly bent over and directed into me. I want to kick and try again, but it's futile to try and move any part of my lifeless, dead weight body.

Fuck, what does he want? Why can't he just tell me what he wants? Money, gold, the package – fuck! – the package. Is it safe? It must be the package he is after. Femi. Femi must be nearby, I am sure he took the makeshift bed on the floor over in the corner. If I can only get his attention, he can fend off this being. Come on, Femi. You must be close by. You should be able to sense someone else is in here.

"HELP!" I scream, but fuck, I realise that the sound of the scream is in my mind and nothing has left my mouth.

The touch on my leg is now travelling. It is definitely a hand; a couple of fingers, sliding slowly up my naked legs. They travel up the outside of my calf, pausing as they reach my knee. The hooded faceless face tilts to the side slightly. In a mocking gesture it seems. I force my eyes shut in an attempt to make myself believe that this is all in my head, all in my twisted imagination and when I open my eyes there will be no one here and I will look over to the floor and see the gentle rise and fall of Femi's chest as he sleeps. In the corner of the room there will be the package, safe and in its own bedding for the night. But fuck, no, as I open my eyes, the figure persists. My dense wooden body is still unable to move of its own free will. My voice is still not capable of forming anything that resonates from my mouth.

I can feel that the hand has rested on my knee, cupping it. It is as if he is waiting for me to open my eyes again so that he can be sure I am taking note of all his actions. His head is still slightly tilted to the side. I look directly at it. I can tell he knows I am looking now, paying attention to what he wanted. It feels as though he nods with appreciation of my effort to pay attention and concentrate on his efforts, as he slowly continues with his hand around my knee, like

I permitted him to do so once I reopened my eyes. I just want this over with now. Whatever this is.

My chest aches. I can feel my lungs filling with the toxin. It's suffocating me. Deep burning pressure twisting through my ribs, causing them to splinter and shatter. Every time I try to get my lungs to fill with air, there is an intense ripping pain that only compares to something unnatural and sinister. This is probably what it feels like to drown, deep in the sea, just being swallowed by the dense layers of the water, just building on top of me. My mouth swallowing the gallons of sea water, filling every aspect of my trachea and bronchioles in my lungs. The lungs cannot expand any further and they want to rip apart, shattering the surrounding rib cage as they grow.

My attention is pulled back to his fingers on my leg. They are tapping lightly in some sort of rhythm along the inner side of my thigh. I am sure he is mocking me by mimicking playing the piano keys on my leg. The way he positions his fingers, it seems he is playing chords. I can feel his thumb and fourth fingers tap together, followed by his second and third fingers in quick succession.

Fuck, he is moving closer into me. This is it. This is the end. I just know it. I need to kick, to scream. I need to do something to get this figure away from me. I can't end like this without even a chance to defend. Without even a fair fight. Not that I am any good at fighting. I thought that was what Femi was for, by my side.

The weight of his hand is heavy on my thigh. Pushing deeper into the muscle. I am aware of the sweat on my legs, creating a pool under his hand. From the sensation of his touch, it is clear he is not wearing any gloves. Which can only mean one thing. He does not give a fuck about getting caught or leaving a trail. This means he must be good at what he does, very confident or just plain stupid. His head moves to within inches of my face. It's there. In direct distance to head-butt, to bite. But I remain powerless. At his absolute submission. I am unable to feel his breath; nothing is coming from the dark hole that is encased by the hood. No eyes to reflect any form of emotion from. No mouth to decipher words from. Just fucking pitch-black.

I feel my thigh tighten under pressure. It's burning now. I am not sure if it's heat or the grip of his vice-like hand. But it's now digging deep. My skin feels tight and twisted under the pressure. Any further pressure and I am sure the skin will breach. I am sure it will tear and the underlying nerves and muscle fibres will become exposed. Damn, that is what is happening. The pain had a slight few seconds' delay, like when you stub your toe on the end of a table and you have a slight second of realisation and then, bang! the pain hits – throbbing in nature. That is what is occurring now. The burning, twisting, cutting and piercing pain, deep within my thigh. I need to scream, I need to let this emotion out. The face gets closer. So close that my nose is almost lost into the abyss of his darkness. I now can't breathe at all. Nothing. No air. Any oxygen has evaporated away from me. My head is now spinning; laying here feels like everything is turning around me, but the face, filling most of my visual field now, stays absolutely still – right there. The high-pitched tinnitus in my ears starts to drown out the silence in the room. My eyelids feel heavy. They feel the need to close. I don't know if it's the toxin he has administered or the trauma occurring to my thigh that is causing my consciousness to fade. Fading away so gradually, but ever so painfully, that I have only just a few minutes left.

There is no more oxygen from my lungs. I know this. I am sure a main artery in my thigh has been severed, allowing the blood to drain away from my lifeless body.

The pressure on my shoulders increases. I can feel a physical touch and presence on both my shoulders. Now I feel my whole body starting to rock and shake side to side. The tinnitus seems to resemble my name. Over and over, I am sure I can hear my name. 'Hugo' is being formed amongst the chaos of my tinnitus. I try and concentrate on the sound. It *is* my name. I can make out the distinctive 'H' of the name and the resting pressure on the letters 'G' and 'O' at the end to sound just like 'GO'.

Fuck. What was that? My face feels a shock. Something so cold, so freezing and so wet.

"HUGO! Wake the fuck up! Open your eyes."

I recognise the voice. My eyes open. I blink repetitively to allow whatever was thrown over my face to leave my eyes. My vision starts to clear. The blurring moves away. I look around at my surroundings. Fuck, I'm confused.

"Hugo, you OK?" I recognise the voice of Femi standing by the side of my bed. His right hand resting on my shoulder and in his left, I can see a half-empty water bottle.

"Take it easy. Breathe, mate. Take a few deep breaths." The instructions from Femi.

I am conscious of my breathing now. Not feeling suffocated. I can get the air into my lungs. I pull my knees up and feel my thigh with my hand. It has a damp feeling of water, but nothing else.

"Femi. What's going on?"

"You tell *me*, mate." I can see his face, a mixture of confusion and concern.

"I… I was…" I start to stutter my response. My mouth is dry despite the water that was thrown over me. Then it dawns on me. I was having a fucking nightmare. *Another* one. Femi looks at me with understanding eyes.

"You woke me up screaming, man. I thought a spider or something had bitten you." Femi's words register as I sit up in the bed and look around at my surroundings again. It's all coming back now. We are on the boat, under deck, on our way to Cairo, up the Nile, with Femi's cousin being our captain on this voyage. I glance over to the corner of the room. The package is sitting on its throne, resting in comfort and safe in nature. I can sense inner relief at the fact that I was only having a nightmare.

"I'm sorry. What was I saying or doing?" I question Femi, as I want to be sure I didn't do or say anything stupid.

"Don't say sorry, man. Not like you did it on purpose. But you were screaming and waving your hands in front of your face, like you were trying to get away from someone or something. The only words I could make out were 'Get away. No, please. Not again'."

Femi moves over to the far corner of the room, gets some towels and throws one over me. I wipe the combination of water and sweat off my face and torso. I can hear the hum of the engine room that is just on the other side of the wall. There is also the soothing hum of the motor and then the metallic pinging of the runner chains on the motor.

"I'm sorry, Femi, it must be the heat and lack of hydration. It gives me strange dreams."

I feel the burning sensation from my neck to my face as I say the words, as I know this is not the first time I have had this dream. It is also not the first time I have discussed this dream with my therapist. Fuck. I thought

I had managed to deal with these subconscious demons hidden away behind the locked doors of my mind. The dark place that I do not want to go to.

"As I said, don't worry about it." Femi yawns as he speaks. I notice it is probably late in the night. "We should try and get back to sleep and rest as much as we can, while we can."

"Yes. Of course." I still feel embarrassed for the nightmare and waking Femi up. "I am just going to get a bit of air on deck. It may help clear my mind in order to sleep in peace."

Femi gives a slight grunt at my sentence and he goes back to his corner of the floor where he has laid his bed for the night. I turn the light off as I leave the room to let the humid night air wash over my sweaty face and close the door behind me. Then I look down and remember I am only wearing my boxers. Fuck.

16

My bloody neck aches. Opening my eyes, I come back to the room, below deck on the boat. It is bright now and the sun is making its way through the small windows over the far side of the room. I am sure the bed was more comfortable when I got into it last night. I can already feel the heat and sweat that lies underneath me, soaking the mattress. Femi has already got up and left the room as I turn and look over to the floor where he was sleeping. The package is still safe in its position in the corner of the room. Sitting up, I notice that the engine's sound is back to its low hum and we are not swaying like we were when the boat was travelling up the Nile. Which means we are stationary. We must be in Cairo.

"Hugo, you up?" Femi knocks on the door.

"Yeh, I'm up. I'm up."

"Come on. We need to get going soon."

All I have been told about Cairo is that we are meeting the curator who has been chosen to take hold of the package. In their presence, I will have my time to finally be with the artefact. With the marvel and wonder that it holds within it. I will have all the time to ensure that my research stacks up and proves my theories. Yeh, fuck all those who laughed at my idea.

"Hugo!"

Shit.

"I'm coming!"

The day shines bright into my eyes as I step onto the deck. I have to use my hand to shield them. The sun bounces off the water like a camera flashes off a mirror. The slight movement of the water's surface creates an illusion of small diamonds floating past.

"Ah, the London gentleman awakens." I hear the joyful voice of Kunlee drift across the deck. Why is he always so happy? "Come, come; join us for coffee and breakfast before you both set off."

I can see he is leaning on the edge of the boat holding a flask in his hand. Femi is looking out to shore beside him. I look around us, to the surrounding shorelines as I walk towards the two. One thing is obvious; I cannot see the density and pollution that I would have associated with Cairo. After all, Cairo is one of the most densely populated cities globally. But, here, where we are anchored, I can see only green lush trees and dunes.

Femi turns to me as I approach.

"How did you sleep, in the end?"

I sense his question is loaded with an underlying curiosity about my nightmare that he witnessed last night.

"All good. Neck is aching from the bed, but a good stretch will sort that out. So, where are we?"

Kunlee pours me a cup of dark, black coffee from his flask.

"Welcome to Cairo." He explains further as he notices me look around the boat again. "We are just to the left of El Saff." He gestures with his free hand across to the shore.

"El Saff?" I question.

Femi cuts in.

"Yes, it's a city just past those dunes. Cairo is about 60 kilometres north from here. We will make the rest of our journey on land."

This is a surprise to me. I was under the impression that we were headed straight into Cairo by boat. From Femi's facial expression, I can tell that he has read my mind.

"We have a few stops to do on the way, as I explained last night." Femi winks to me as he speaks, out of the gaze of Kunlee.

"Oh yes, I forgot; sure. Yes, this is a great spot to disembark." I can feel my words overplaying the situation and I decide to take a sip of the coffee before saying something that I am not supposed to. But I need to understand why the plan has changed.

I burn the roof of my mouth with the hot coffee. I can see that Femi is already done with his coffee and checking his watch for the time. I look down at my wrist and see that I left my watch in the room. There is a tan line showing where my watch rested on my wrist.

"Well, it's a shame we did not get to spend more time together. I could have told you all the embarrassing stories about Femi when he was growing up." Kunlee lets out a laugh as he looks over to Femi and, in return, Femi rolls his eyes and kisses his teeth in jest.

"Come on, Hugo. We should get our bits together and get going." Femi pushes off the edge of the boat rail and makes his way back to our room.

"Thanks for the great coffee; it's stronger than anything I have had back in London."

"Ha, London has nothing on the real coffee houses of

the continent of Africa." Again, the roar of laughter from Kunlee.

I follow Femi back into the room and he is already gathering all our belongings back into the two rucksacks.

"Femi, what was that all about? I thought we were going into Cairo with the boat." Femi does not turn around while I speak. His back is facing me and is bent over the bed, concentrating on getting all the items into the bag.

"Femi!"

He stops doing what he is doing at the sound of his name.

"Close the door behind you."

As instructed, I walk over to the far end of the room, where the package is resting on the chair. I can now see the contraction on the face of Femi as he looks up at me and rests his hands on his hips and lets out a sigh.

"Hugo. I am not sure how safe it is being on the boat into Cairo."

I am conscious of the look of confusion plastered over my face at that comment.

"But you reassured me that we could trust your cousin."

Femi takes a step closer to me. The sun catches his eyes as it beams into the room from the tiny windows above my head.

"Greed and money can change the intent of any man."

This was a worrying comment from Femi. I struggled to work out if it was intended directly as a reference to himself, his cousin or myself.

"What are you talking about, Femi? I really don't understand. Are we in danger?"

"I don't fully know the other crew members on the boat. Kunlee assures me that they are known to him and trustworthy, but…" He pauses as though what he will say will confirm the worst case. I hate it when he gets like this. Like he needs to tiptoe around me to protect me from his thoughts and words.

"But what, exactly, Femi?" My words come out harsher than they should have.

Femi turns back to finish packing the bags on the bed. Fuck this; I need to know what is going on in his head. I try and reach over and grab the bag from the bed, but the contents spill back. Not a great choice of action – there are boxer shorts, toothpaste, socks and a couple of t-shirts now exposed on the bed. At least it got Femi's attention.

"Look. I have trusted you ever since London. Coming out here… how we got the package out and with us now. I mean, what the hell? We are basically on the run with what seems to be stolen property. The way you have been acting, it is like our lives are at stake here from anyone who wants to get to that thing." I am breathless from talking with the build-up of adrenaline. The sweat drips down my neck, making its way down the middle of my back, along my spine.

"You have been acting more anxious and distracted since you went to investigate if someone was following us back there in the bush. I can tell from your face and how tense you have been since then." Femi avoids eye contact while I speak and is still focused on the contents on the bed. "You at least owe me a bit of the truth here and exactly what I have got myself into."

I am nearly panting now with my breaths. I let my words hang there between us.

Femi drops his shoulders. He looks worn out by my words. He sits on the edge of the bed, again with his back to me, and places his head in his hands.

"Hugo, I did not think it would be this difficult. Had I have known, perhaps I would not have asked you to come all this way out here."

His voice sounds sincere and with the emotion of someone who cares. It has softness to it. A fragile softness. My attention is drawn to someone walking outside our room, on the deck. After what Femi said, I need to be conscious of the volume of my voice.

"Femi, I don't think anyone could have known how all this has turned out. I mean, I was supposed to be here to offer my intellectual abilities, not to be on an Indiana Jones adventure. But all I ask is that you just keep me in the loop of the situation at all times."

I spot my cheap watch on the edge of the bed and one part of me is comforted by the fact that it has been with me since London. I reach for it and fasten it on my wrist, covering the perfect-fitting tan line.

"I know, Hugo, and I am sorry for being very cloak-and-dagger about certain aspects, but I am trying to let you just concentrate on the one thing you need to be concentrating on," he says while nodding towards the corner where the package is, before continuing, "while I try and maintain the safety for us to get to the curator."

This curator is someone that I need to know more about as I have not been told much and I have not pushed to ask more either.

"Look, fine; OK, I get it. You protect us, while I can concentrate on what I am supposed to be doing. So, how far is Cairo from here and how do you propose we get there?"

He turns his head towards me and I can see his smile

return. In those sentences I reinstate the trust I have in him, which I hope is not a misjudgement on my part.

"It is probably a two-hour car ride to where we need to get to. We would have gained good ground overnight by travelling on the boat. I highly doubt that anyone was able to follow our tracks and so I think we are safe to find transport to get us to Cairo."

"Well, that sounds like a plan then, Femi. So, who gets the pleasure of carrying our friend for this leg of the journey?" I look over to the package while I fiddle with my watch strap and am aware that Femi is still not giving me the full picture. My gut feeling is giving me concerned vibes.

17

Before

Femi was already waiting for me, patiently as always, at the place we decided to meet for lunch. Although we have now seen each other every day for a good few hours each day, I have not and he has not suggested coming to the apartment to do our meetings or work. I can only imagine that this is him wishing to maintain a boundary and respect my personal life outside of what we are doing with this project, contract, research; whatever it is. All I know of where he is staying is that it is some hotel in Westminster. He, again, has not given away any more than that.

The small, intimate coffee/lunch place is just off Seven Dials in Covent Garden. I spot Femi sitting along the back booth as I walk through the door, which has two small, square tables pulled together. He has his coat on the back of a chair in front of him, saving the seat, no doubt. He makes the booth and table look like a small Lego set as he sits there, with his left arm resting on the seat next to him. He catches my stare as I walk in and beckons me over with a wave of his hand – like I would miss seeing him.

"In all my time in London I don't think I have ever noticed this place," I remark as I place my bag on the chair next to Femi and take a seat opposite him. The place is busy with a young crowd of people. Most seem like tourists with various shopping bags placed down beside them. There is a life-sized tree in the middle of the room, with branches and leaves radiating across the ceiling like a fan.

"What would you like to drink?" he asks while Femi gets the attention of the staff.

"Just a flat white and tap water to get going. Thanks, Femi."

Femi orders a green tea. I cannot help but be reminded of an ironic comedy scene of this big, strong man holding a delicate green tea in his hands. Sipping away with his pinky sticking up from his hand.

"We have a lot to get on with. The timing has been brought forward for our travels."

I look at Femi while I remove my coat. I can feel how hot I am sitting here under all the reflective lights. There are a series of mirrors on the wall behind Femi and I catch my reflection in them and notice how ragged and worn I look. I really need to get a grip on my sleeping patterns. Perhaps I will get some herbal teas on the way home that are supposed to help with sleep.

"'Travels' – sorry, what do you mean, 'our travels'?" As I ask Femi, I am trying to recall if I was told anything about requiring to travel as part of this.

"Yes. The artefact of particular concern to us. The artefact that your expertise is needed on may be on the move soon and we must get to it before it moves location, as it has taken us a lot of time to finally locate it and we cannot risk it going AWOL again."

I sense a very businesslike tone in Femi's voice. There seems to be an urgency and assertiveness to him today.

Our drinks arrive, as I am about to poke Femi further

into this travel aspect. My flat white in a nice yellow cup with red saucer, while Femi's green tea has an elaborate teapot and drainer placed on the table, with what looks like a fine china cup. This is still playing into my imagination of a comedy sketch of him drinking the tea.

I wait for the staff member to move away from the table before continuing.

"Where do we need to travel to?"

"We will get to that later. But let's get down to the research aspects you have pulled together and brought along with you today so we can make sure we are all on the same page." Femi concentrates on the teapot while he speaks. "I am sure everything you have stacks up, but obviously, my boss just wants me to have sight of it as there is a lot at stake here. I am sure you understand. Don't you, Hugo?"

He stops looking at the teapot and locks eyes with me. I do not like this Femi version, I have decided.

"Pass me over my bag," I ask. With what seems like no effort at all, Femi smoothly hands over my bag from the seat next to him. He makes space on the tables. No wonder he organised two tables to be pulled together side by side. This is like a study session at university.

"Well, now I know that this is all about the *Sunflowers* series of paintings that Vincent did. I have got all the research I have on that aspect of his life." I pull out my papers and notebooks that I managed to get together from my disorganised chaotic filing system at home. As I place them out on the table, I feel slightly embarrassed at how messy they all look and how my handwriting needs special training to read and make sense of. "So, how do you want to do this? Is there anything in particular we need to focus on here?"

"Well, let's just start from where you think is important. I am sure that I know only the basic facts about the *Sunflowers*. Let's see what I can learn from you and then I will steer you towards where we need to get to."

Hearing that from Femi makes me think that I am still being tested. But, Femi has been so convincing over these last few days and I have trusted him.

He takes a sip of his tea while I try to navigate the papers on the table and make a start.

"Well, some of the background I have done on Vincent is important to know and understand concerning the *Sunflowers* that were painted." I am so sure that I know all the facts without relying on reading any printed material, but I want Femi to know that there is real evidence behind what I am saying.

"So, I am sure you know why and when the *Sunflowers* were painted." There was no reaction from Femi; he just sat, relaxed, leaning back in the booth like he was in the middle of a Sunday afternoon movie, without a care in the world. "The *Sunflowers* collection actually consists of seven paintings in all. Vincent painted them between 1888 and 1889. Four of them were painted in August of 1888 and three were painted in January 1889."

Femi lets a little chuckle out.

"See, I have learnt something new already. I had no idea how many of these were painted."

I ruffle through my notebook pages and open it up at a double-page spread where I found the *Sunflowers'* images and stuck them in the notebook. I turn it around so Femi can see them. He places his finger on the images and traces them like he is remembering a past he once knew. He turns the page and then back again.

"There are only five pictures here. Do you have images of the other two?"

"Well, that's the mystery and the pull of these paintings. Two of the seven have not been seen for decades." I look at Femi's reaction and he seems unmoved by what I have just said. Then it hit me. This is about the two *Sunflowers* that have not been seen in public for all this time.

"So, Vincent painted these in preparation for his friend, another artist called Gauguin. Vincent looked up to this person and wanted to impress him so that they could work together to create several pieces and so that his brother, Theo, could sell them." I take a sip of my flat white and check Femi is still showing interest in this, which, from his facial expression, I can tell he is. I continue.

"Vincent moved to the famous Yellow House in Arles, where he started painting the *Sunflowers*. He had to work quickly to paint them as he was using real sunflowers as the subjects and so the paintings capture how the flowers faded throughout the day. This resembles what happens to us in emotion."

I get the notebook back from Femi to find a particular note I want to show him. I wanted to be sure of some of the dates.

"In 1921, it is reported that one of the paintings was bought by a wealthy Japanese collector." I find the page in the notebook. "Here it is. There is a ledger that I was able to find from an art auction house in Paris that confirms the sale and transport of the painting to Japan in July 1921." In the pile of papers, I get the photocopy of the ledger and hand it over to Femi. He studies it with concentration, narrowing his eyes. It seems he can read French as the ledger is all in that language.

"So, this confirms that this is proof that one of the paintings left France and went to Japan in 1921, in particular, on July 18th 1921?"

"Yes, Femi. That is correct."

"Which one was it that was sold to this Japanese person?"

"Well, this is where the art world is divided in its opinion."

"Hugo, it is not the art world's opinion that we are concerned with. It is your research and inferences that concern us."

Feels like I just got told off. I can slightly feel my face blushing at that sharp comment from Femi.

"Well, the first two paintings in the *Sunflowers* series are the ones that have not been seen in public. The special aspect about these first two paintings is that he used the colour blue as opposed to yellow that dominates the other five paintings."

I pull out another piece of paper from the pile on the table. It is a copy of a letter from Vincent to his brother, Theo.

"Here, look at this extract from a letter that Vincent wrote to his brother at the time." I spin the page around for Femi to read.

He reads out loud: "'The whole thing will be a symphony in blue and yellow'."

He places the paper back on the pile on the table, interlocks his fingers together and rests his chin on them. He raises his eyebrow and begins with,

"Well…"

I sigh. I know what he wants to hear.

"The first two paintings – the *Sunflowers* that were done in blue. One was reported as destroyed in World War Two when the Americans bombed Japan. The second blue *Sunflowers* was reported to have been sold to another Japanese family and has been kept in a private collection."

"Would you gentlemen like any food?" I am startled by the voice from behind me. I look at the reflection in the mirror, behind Femi, and see a member of staff standing at my shoulder with a notebook and pencil in hand.

Femi takes the lead, as always.

"Sure, could we see the menu, please?" while flashing one of his smiles. Although he has the scar on the side of his face, the smile complements it to some degree. The waiter pulls out two menus, hands them to us and walks away saying,

"I will come back in a couple of minutes to take your order."

Femi puts the menus back on the table and his smile disappears while he turns his attention back to me.

"Where do you think both of these paintings are, Hugo?"

"I know they are still in existence. There have been rumours that the paintings left Japan before the bombing occurred. But no one ever followed this line of thought through or indeed found any real concrete evidence of this."

"Apart from you; right, Hugo?"

I reach for my bag again.

"There were many Japanese families of wealth in that period, but not many were interested in the art from European artists. You see, that was a time when Japanese art and culture was starting to make a global breakthrough and so the wealth of Japan was invested into its own."

"I sense a 'but' coming along here…"

"Yes, Femi. But as this picture and document shows, there was one particular family that saw European art, in particular, Vincent van Gogh art, as important statements for the creative society."

I let Femi study the black and white faded photograph I handed him. His facial expression changes in that instance as he focuses on what he can see in the mirror's reflection in the photograph. He pulls the picture closer to his eyes.

"The paintings in the reflection of the mirror."

"Yes, Femi, you see–"

"They *are* – they are the *Sunflowers*."

"They are indeed the two, blue, missing *Sunflowers* paintings, side by side."

"There is another interesting fact about this photograph. The family that is standing in the picture. The children in the picture. The young girl and her brother are aged around eight to ten."

"Yes, Hugo, they look very proud Japanese children, smiling and wearing…"

Femi stops mid-sentence. He pulls the photograph closer to his eyes.

"The t-shirts on the children. They… they–"

"Yes, Femi." I can see that Femi has now understood the significance of what my research has been centred on and how I have been so confident that the two blue *Sunflowers* van Gogh paintings are safe in the world after World War Two.

"The t-shirts on the children…. They indicate the time that The Beatles, the British band, was coming to an end as Paul McCartney was leaving them. This occurred in 1970."

Femi just stared at the photograph, in silence.

"You gentlemen ready to order?"

I looked over to my right and noticed the young person standing at my side, with pen and paper ready to take our order. There was an interesting tattoo on the dorsum of her hand, a snake of some sort and her nails were painted in all different colours. I give a big sigh of contentment and smile.

"I am starving. What do you recommend?"

18

Now

I think I am done with this continent now. It is hot, dry, humid and all manner in-between. My feet ache and have blisters. My lips are chapped and I cannot stop licking them to keep them wet but, as I discovered earlier, that in turn dries them even further. I have red heat rashes all over my skin and areas of itchy, infected insect bites that I scratch with obsession during my sleep. I scratch at any given moment, but it is worse at night when trying to rest as my attention is drawn to them. I draw blood from some of the infected lesions and often wake with dried blood mixed with dirt under my fingernails. I thought we would have some reprieve once we were on the boat, but that was short-lived as now we have more journeying over land to reach the location in Cairo. However, I suppose the good thing about this last leg of the journey is that Femi thinks it's safe enough for us to get transport of some manner – a car, perhaps.

We said our goodbyes to Kunlee and the rest of the crew once we had gathered all our belongings from below the deck. Our normal checks for the safety of the package casing was done and attached to the back of Femi securely. I have been trying to settle my inner unrest with all this.

I also keep having this horrible anxiety inside that Femi is going to leave me at some point. It's giving me dark behavioural thoughts flooding back to me. What did Fiona say to me about trauma inherited from our parents and generations before that? *"Regardless of how we see our parents, they are part of us. Rejecting them only creates more suffering for us."* Umm, somehow I beg to differ with that statement. It's precisely that trauma that I was exposed to that is the cause of all my current toxic behaviours. Behaviours that cause me to create situations in my mind that make everything around me tumble down.

"We should be able to pick up a main road if we follow this beaten track inland, according to my cousin." Femi is taking the lead ahead and I follow in tow, carrying the bags of our belongings. I do feel slightly more rested than the previous evening. Perhaps the slight sway of the boat at night helped in getting me off to sleep, regardless of that fucking nightmare situation.

"Tell me more about this curator we are meeting. Do you have any background on them? I mean, do they belong to a particular museum or art restoration service?" I know I will not get much back from Femi on this as he would have told me already about all the details by now if he had wanted to. I have a suspicion that his boss has ordered him not to give too much away.

Femi strides ahead of me. The ground is flat and not demanding as we continue on the beaten track.

"I think he works for some arts committee of Egypt. But I could be making that up. I am not sure, to be honest."

As I suspected, not much given away from Femi at this stage. My sixth sense is telling me that Femi knows so much more than he is letting on.

There is no harm in pushing a bit more to see if Femi can crack.

"Is there a name you have or do you know where we are meeting them, at least?"

Femi takes another few big strides before coming to a stop. He straightens his back and stretches his arms on either side of him. Slowly, he turns on the spot to face me. He looks disappointed.

"Is this another trust thing rearing its head, Hugo?"

Fuck, how dare he! Is he really using my issues against me here?

"What do you mean? Why do you feel that I do not have a right to know where we are going, who we are meeting? I mean, for fuck's sake, Femi, this is bloody stressful on all accounts."

"Look, Hugo, I know how difficult this is and also I understand how this is all a shock to the system. What happened back there in Luxor, I mean, it was not supposed to go down that way. But it is what it is now and we are where we are. The gravity of the situation is like this because of what this discovery means, not just to the art world, but to a wider community of individuals and groups."

I study Femi's body language, head to toe, as he stands there ahead of me in the sun, surrounded by the green bush and sand dunes with the heat engulfing everything around us from the sun's rays. He looks as calm and collective as ever.

"You knew, didn't you? You knew what was going to happen in Luxor, with the painting." I give Femi an accusation that I so want him to rebut. To deny all knowledge that it was going to go down that way.

"I didn't take you in with me because I was trying to protect you, Hugo."

I cannot help but let out a bout of laughter.

"Protect me! Protect me, Femi? I mean, fucking hell! What were you going to do when we got here? The only thing you protected me from was being exposed to your lies."

We stood there. Like a Western showdown. Neither of us wanting to look away or back down. I have both my hands full with the bags. Femi is standing tall, chest puffed out, shoulders bursting out from the straps of the package on his back. A flight of birds swoops overhead and all we hear is the slight faint patter of their wings. There is still the calming sound of the rippling water hitting the shoreline drifting in the air.

Femi drops his shoulders. He lets out a sigh and walks over to me, dragging his feet in the sand. "Come, let's sit for a moment to talk."

"I prefer to stand, Femi. What do you want to say?" I may sound confident in my voice, but I am absolutely petrified inside. So out of my depth and comfort zone.

"Suit yourself, but I am sitting down. This gets heavier and heavier each time I carry it."

He finds a flat area on the sand to sit, his legs bent in front of him and he keeps his back as straight as he can, hooking his arms around his knees for stability.

My legs are aching and my neck is still aching from the position I slept in. I could so do with resting on the floor as Femi is, but I will hold my ground.

"I had no idea that we would need to..." Femi hesitates and so I help him finish the sentence.

"...be as cloak-and-dagger as we have been."

"Yes, Hugo. Things are not as straightforward as I had anticipated. But, that does not mean anything is wrong or that we are not on the right path with all this. It's just that the way to get there has become just a little more complicated."

This would be a good time to have a lie detector test to hand. Femi is looking directly up at me as he speaks. His eyes make direct contact with me and they seem to have honesty encased in them. He seems sincere in his words. However, I have had that same look in the past from people I thought I trusted. From people I thought wanted me for me. From people I tried to open up to and be myself around. I saw that same look from her and she burnt me to the core.

"But, surely you would have known where the painting was, who had it, the fact that it was on that place you went? I mean, I was under the impression that I was to view the painting and give my appraisal there and then."

The sweat is now making its way down the side of my face. I can feel it from my temples, along my jawline, to my neck. Every now and then, I hear the buzz of a fly, most likely a mosquito, around my ears. Whenever the sound stops, I get paranoid that it has landed on my skin and is having a meal.

"The people I work for, they..." Femi looks down into his lap, "...they are the ones that call all the shots. I get told certain aspects about the... well, I suppose we can call it a mission, as it unfolds."

Fuck it. I am tired. I sit on the floor next to Femi, but that does not mean I am giving him the upper hand. I am in control here.

"So, in London, when we discussed aspects of the missing *Sunflowers*, did you know then that you would have to put me in this situation?"

Femi sighs. He raises his head out of his pathetic 'feel pity for me' posture and looks in my direction.

"I knew it was going to be challenging, but not like this. Not so that it ends up with…"

He does not finish his sentence. I know he wants to say something. I know he is bursting to tell me something of great importance.

"Hugo, I am doing all I can to protect you. I will continue to do that until the end of this. You have my word. But I need you to trust me. I need you to remember the trust we built in London. That is important here."

I always thought to myself that if someone told me to trust them it usually meant the exact opposite, that they were creating a manipulating environment to lure me into a false sense of security. This is what I am programmed to think and feel. This is what my instincts do, they reach out from inside and tear through the surface to slap me in the face to wake up to reality.

"Well, let me trust you in getting us to Cairo in one piece and I would prefer not to by foot. I don't think my feet want to take any further steps. So let's find some sort of safe vehicle to get us there."

Femi smiles in my direction and no further words are needed at this moment as I have to stay calm until I can work this out in my own head first. I need to keep the irrational thought processes at bay for now.

19

Before

"Thank you for fitting me in early this week." Fiona opens the door to her room and welcomes me in. I still have not got out of the habit of feeling uncomfortable when greeting her at the start of our sessions. Never seems easy to shake hands, hug or just nod as I walk in. I think, subconsciously, I always have to have my hands full with items so it takes the hug and handshake out of the equation. As always, it's a reading book and a bag in each hand.

"It is fine, Hugo. Some of my clients are out of London and so I have more availability and am able to juggle things around."

I take my normal position on the sofa.

"So, you mentioned in your message that you may need to travel overseas for a while. Anywhere nice?"

Fiona opens up with a nice ice-breaker.

"Not entirely sure as yet, but it may be next week that I need to travel and so I was keen to get an extra session in with you this week."

Fiona sits back in her chair.

"There is obviously still the option of face time or phone sessions while you are travelling, if you feel that is something you want to explore."

The word 'explore' from her is a very delicate way of putting that I still have some issues with face time and photos in general. Something that only recently surfaced from my subconscious as the root cause of this.

"I know. Perhaps, depending on the time difference and if it can work, telephone may be good. But let's hold off on the virtual face time options just yet, if that's OK."

"Of course," she says as she lets out one of those reassuring, comforting smiles, which tells me she understands and that there is no need for further discussion on the subject.

"So, how have you been since our last session?"

The question that acts as a marker for me to retrace my mind over the last few days.

"It has not been too bad. I have been keeping focused and busy with this new project I have."

"Oh yes, the Vincent van Gogh one. How exciting." Fiona seems genuinely pleased for me.

"Yes, and as part of it I have someone to work alongside me with the project. In fact, I am meeting him after this session to continue with some of the planning, before we travel."

I know Fiona will bite at this. I would not have mentioned that I am working alongside someone if I did not feel there was something about those dynamics that I was either uncomfortable with or something that I wanted to pick at and get Fiona's direction on. As I have learned, Fiona's way of asking more in relation to something with me sometimes means she says nothing at all.

I could never fully understand why, at times, Fiona would not say anything. At first, obviously I thought it was because she wanted to give me time and space to get used to speaking about myself, which I am sure is also part of the reason. But after doing some reading around the subject, I learnt that it is her way of getting *me* to open up my non-declarative memory. This is where all the traumatic experiences are stored in my brain. The traumatic events were so powerful at the time, that I lost words to describe them at the moment they occurred to me. Hence, because I could not put words to the events, they now revisit me in adulthood in other ways. This is the core language that Fiona is getting me now to learn. I am onto her.

"He is helping me get all my research together and making sure everything makes sense. I am also enjoying…" This is more difficult than I thought it would be.

"Yes, Hugo? What are you also enjoying?" she prompts gently.

I can feel my shoulders tighten and, as if on autopilot, my hand reaches for my neck. I suppose this is another one of those physical adaptive behaviours I have learned in replacing my core language.

"I am enjoying having a friendship with this person. He seems like he is really interested in what I have to say. Not just about the work, but in general, like he takes an interest in me as a person."

"That is a great feeling. Why are you so hesitant to allow it to happen? What is your worry? Where has that thought taken you?"

Thinking of my response is a way to casually glance at the clock resting over to my left.

"I suppose I am afraid of being let down. Of letting my trust open up and to be perhaps let down by a person whom I saw as a friend."

"So, shall we take a few steps back, just for a second?

You have mentioned a friend called Charlie in the past. You have said this is a true friend who has been there for you unconditionally in the past. Correct?"

I nod in agreement.

"And he has not let you down, right? I mean, there is not anything that Charlie has done in which you feel your trust aspects in him are misplaced."

"No. Charlie has been an absolute rock to me. I mean, he really stepped up recently with *her*, also." I dare not mention her name in my safe space here. I can tell Fiona was very protective of me when I first explained the situation with *her*.

"Yes, I remember when he spent a weekend down here with you in London when you were feeling fragile a while ago."

I still carry that label from the cigar that Charlie and I had at the club on 10 Manchester Street. That was my first experience of having a cigar and, actually, there was no coughing, as I had feared. Charlie and I ordered Trinidad cigars and spent a few hours there speaking about anything and everything apart from any triggers that could take me back to that dark place. Every time I open my card wallet I see that cigar label poking out and it reminds me that at the time I was feeling dark, but that there was hope in a true friend who wanted nothing in return.

"So, Hugo, tell me; what is there to fear in this other person? Has he not acted like Charlie so far? The same qualities, the same type of behaviour?"

I picture Femi's facial features as I take my time over Fiona's question. Femi's kind eyes and gentle smile. The way he has always been patient with me when it comes to my timing or my train of thought when I need a moment every now and then. How he senses that I am not always so focused or settled. He shows genuine empathy. Also, just like Charlie, he says it how it is and is direct with me at times when it is needed.

"You are right. He does have the similar traits, well, I mean, he makes me feel in a similar way that Charlie does."

"There you go. Just by saying it aloud, the words, you have relaxed your posture." I look up as Fiona says this and I notice for the first time that I am sitting back in the sofa, relaxed, without my hands high up at my neck.

"So, I think your homework will be just to allow this friendship to flow where it goes, before you feel committed on any aspect. At the moment it feels like your defence walls are coming up too early, but you have a good baseline and sounding board in the nature of Charlie, so you can compare and contrast this as your safety."

I hear her words and let them sink in. I could never remember some areas of my sessions when I left Fiona and I always wondered why that was. Then I realised that I was so intensely focused on using the full 50 minutes efficiently that I would jump from one emotion to the other to get Fiona's take on my thoughts. Now, I take my time to join all the dots before moving on.

"So, my concern is whether I will repeat the behaviours that triggered in my relationship with her, in this situation also."

Fiona takes a deep breath.

"Hugo," she begins. I feel she is going to tell me off, perhaps. "There were a lot of projections going on with her. There were triggers all over the place and it took you straight back to the traumas. You need to understand that because of how you rejected your past, your parents, those emotions, those behaviours that you shut away, they remain in your unconscious and they come out in projections in those around you. You attracted certain people around you, in relationships, that mirrored those same behaviours. It was because you did not have the spoken words and language to heal those events that your unconscious attracted those traits in others. But it kept you punishing yourself and, in reality, this is the way you need to find the core language in now allowing it to heal."

Fuck.

"But I acted so bad and treated her so bad. I mean, my projections to her were just so harsh."

"Did you not apologise? Did you not explain that you recognised your behaviours? Did you not make a promise to yourself to work on you and to be gentle to you and focus on healing this now and hence working so much with me, consistently?"

The questions from Fiona all had the same answer.

"Yes."

"So, she is an adult and I am sure she is hurt and disappointed in you, but you are not innately bad – never think that. You recognised your shortcomings and are now doing the work. I hope one day she understands that aspect and if she does not, you need to see that trigger as something that you have learnt from and become a better version of you – the real version of you and not the version that everyone else expects you to be."

I know I have not ventured this far into my self-worth and development journey in the past, but the more I unravel it with Fiona, the more complex and never-ending it seems.

"What if I am never going to get to a stage where I can stop this cycle I am in? I mean, the sabotaging behaviour I have. At times I do not even know I am doing it." I am sure this sentence was supposed to stay in my head and not form words out here. The words of self-doubt have been voiced many times here with Fiona, who reassures me each time, but I worry that she will get tired of me continuing to see failure in myself.

"Be gentle. It is only recently that your memories are starting to open up. I know it is a bumpy ride at present, but these bumps will smooth out in time. You are now starting to link your current behaviours and fears with the deep hidden memories of the past. Your brain would not allow this to occur if you are not ready."

I let the words fill the space between us. I let them sit on the sofa next to me. I allow them to perch on the bookshelf to my right. The words dangle their legs on the small coffee table by the door.

"I am afraid."

"What, Hugo? What scares you most right now?"

"I have nightmares. She held me once when I had one. I laid in her arms on her chest once. I felt safe. I am afraid that I will always push everyone away. I am afraid that the shadows will always win."

I feel my throat tighten. My pulse quickens. The room feels like it is closing in on me. Every object in here resembles accusing eyes directed at me. I feel like I am lying here naked and baring my darkest emotions for all to mock.

Fiona has softness to her voice as she leans forward slightly.

"It's OK, Hugo. Remember, you cannot get hurt if you

do not make a sound and you cannot be lost if you are unable to be found."

I glance at the clock to my left; 50 minutes are up.

The toilet downstairs near the reception of the building where Fiona has her office becomes my sanctuary for a few minutes after the session. I feel slightly more vacant; yes, that is probably the right word to describe how I feel. It is always difficult to know how much progress has been made in the session immediately afterwards. This will be the first time I will not get to see Fiona physically face to face for a while due to the travelling. I'm not going to sugar-coat this, but it scares the shit out of me not having my regular safe space with her, in person. I wonder if I am in danger of being too co-dependent on her, but this is part of the process that I have been reassured about. To allow the safety of the dynamics play out and then eventually have the same dynamics repeated out there, in the wide dangerous world. I just need to make sure that I do not freak out with Femi now. I need to believe in him, in his trust, in the way he wants to support me in this task and also in the fact that he is a genuine person. Otherwise, I risk destroying that rapport between us, which in this case, could be more futile than I realise.

OK, game on with positivity, as I am meeting Femi in exactly… fuck! I am late.

20

Now

I left the negotiations to Femi as we came across the main road; well, what seemed to be the main road. It was a dirt track that appeared to wind on forever into the distance. As we cleared the bush, Femi was able to flag down a passing car and after about two minutes of conversation, we were given a ride in the direction that we were travelling. It was an open backed pick-up truck where Femi and I sat at the rear. We were surrounded by buckets of construction tools. Not those of a main contractor, rather those of a handyman. The sun shone down hard on us. Femi, as usual, was not fazed at all with the sun's heat, whereas I was moving all over the place to try and keep as much of the sun away from my skin. A useless attempt.

"How did you convince him to give us a ride?"

Femi is sitting opposite me, just to the left.

"Easy, Hugo. Money, obviously. What else would get a stranger to help another stranger out?"

I am sure I can see the stress of the journey beginning to show on the face of Femi now. His eyes are wearier than they were in London and he has lost that calming expression that he wore so effortlessly. I sense that he perhaps wants to be left with his own thoughts, but I need the reassurance of conversation to keep me safe here.

"So, will he get us all the way into Cairo?" I watch Femi from the side of my eyes. He is looking out to the surrounding landscape, which is made up of sand dunes and islands of trees. There is the odd single-storey building now and then, but few and far between – nothing complicated, more of a farm house structure.

"He will get us near enough. We will hopefully be within walking distance once we get there. It will probably take us two hours from here. Better than walking, hey. I don't think your boots are doing your feet any favours at the moment."

I look down at my boots. They still seem in good shape, but Femi is right. They are heavy and too insulating, which is not helping protect my feet in this heat. This damn heat. I wish Femi had taken time with me in London to get me kitted out with the appropriate attire for this climate.

"Well, if we have two hours, may as well get comfortable." I unlace my boots and put them to the far corner to let them air. Out of one of the bags, I remove a t-shirt and place it over my head to keep the sun away. Femi checks on the package again while it rests along the back of the driver's cabin.

"Your boss. The one you mentioned you met in the hotel you worked in. The one who approached you and offered you the job." Femi gives no reaction at my words. "I am sure I have met him. Well, not met him, seen him." This gets his attention.

"Really? Where and when and how?" Femi's voice jumps a bit as the vehicle stumbles over a rock.

"Back in London. I was visiting the gallery. Well, actually, went to view one of van Gogh's *Sunflowers*.

The way you described him and how he dressed, I saw the exact same person in the gallery at that time."

"Ummm." Femi leans back and looks ahead in thought. "Did he approach you at all?"

"No. He was passing, in one of the rooms at the gallery. I would not have taken any notice if it weren't for the very distinctive outfit he was wearing. Bit of a coincidence, don't you think?"

Femi did not reply. Studying his face, I could tell he was trying to understand what answer to give, if any. I genuinely believe that Femi did not know that that guy was there when I was there. Femi looks as baffled as me.

"I do not think it was a coincidence. I gather he knew you were there. He must have followed you." Femi's voice has an air of disappointment in it.

"Why do you think he did not approach me himself that day?"

"That is what I am wondering myself," Femi sighs. "I was under the impression that I was the only one to make contact with you and to be the link and, hence, to keep everyone else out of sight."

The sun has shifted as the direction of the truck weaves through the road. I have to continuously alter the position of the t-shirt on my head to keep under some shade. I am soaking in sweat again.

"Perhaps he just wanted to see who I was or if I was dedicated to the research." I can tell I am making excuses to make Femi feel less disappointment. I always have taken on everyone else's moods before my own. Another empathic trait that has caused me pain in life, as I see it as a way for people to validate and accept me if I can show I can fix them. But then, once they do not need fixing or I am unable to fix them or, in most cases, they do not need me to play that role, I see the red flags of abandonment. Another mental note to continue to work on this with Fiona when I get back home.

"We have full water bottles, right? From the boat." Femi changes the subject and reaches for the bag out of his range. I open it for him, fish out a full bottle and throw it over.

"What happened back in Luxor..? When we got the painting I assumed that old guy would have known about that all along."

Femi ceases swigging from the bottle and offers it to me. I shake my head; he replaces the lid and places the bottle down by his side. He keeps his massive hand resting on the top of the bottle.

"I was told it would be difficult to get to view the painting from the outset. But, it was only once we arrived, in Luxor, did I fully understand the gravity of that statement from him," Femi reveals with a reluctant tone to his voice.

This gives me some comfort that Femi was also in the blind with certain details, but it also gives me concern to understand what else we do not know.

"What do you mean when you say you were told 'it would be difficult to view the painting from the outset'? I thought it was all above board and organised before we left London." Femi does not respond to this. I can only assume that I would not like the answer, so I continue. "And I take it the 'Germans', as you put them, are the ones hunting *us* for the painting now. Is it them who you got it from? Back there in Luxor."

There was still nothing coming back from Femi. I am sure he heard me. There is a lot of noise from the road and the wind rushing past our ears, but not enough for him to not fully hear me. He doesn't want to answer my direct questions because he knows I will not like the answers he gives.

"Femi."

"Look, Hugo, there are just so many complicated moving parts to this. Many of which it's best you do not know so that it does not distract you from your purpose here."

I can feel my insides boil with anger towards Femi now.

"My 'purpose'. Well, my *purpose* was not to be dragged through all manner of conditions here. How the fuck do you think I am feeling right now? None of this was explained to me at the outset. My so-called *purpose* was far from what all this entailed."

My voice had grown louder and I can feel myself getting increasingly irritated at Femi, at this truck, at this heat – the fucking heat.

I watch Femi as he looks out into no direction in particular. I know he wants to tell me more, but something holds him back. Have I been wrong with all the trust I have placed in him? I can feel myself running back to the place of safety. That inner wounded child about to have a tantrum. Fuck, I can't do that out here. It's irrational to think I can behave that way here. I mean, where do I have to run? I cannot cause the dynamics and then run and hide, like I always do. How did Fiona teach me to deal with moments like this, going forward? Think, Hugo, think; what did she say?

"I will explain all. I promise, Hugo, I will. You have my word. The reason why this has become so complicated is that…" He pauses. The road is bumpier now and I can feel my head nodding with the contour of the road. I feel like one of those spring back dolls that move for hours if you push them.

"I guess this part is all becoming new to me, also." Femi looks at me directly now while he speaks. "I did not know that the painting would attract so much attention while it is with us. I also did not know about the arrangements, well, lack of arrangements in Luxor."

"You are not going to tell me exactly what happened there, are you? Did you…" I do not want to ask in case the answer is a 'yes' from him. If, indeed, the answer is 'yes' then we're fucked.

"Did you steal it from there?"

The sentence stays where it is, between our locked eyes. Our heads jolting to the road, but our gaze is fixed on each other. I see his jaw clench and his scar come to life momentarily while this happens. His fingers are rubbing against each other. He is rattled. Damn, Femi, do not let me down, do not bring your walls down; I need you to maintain the upper hand here. I need you to tell me all is under your control and you will ensure that this will all come to a safe conclusion. Don't fucking let me down, Femi. Not now, not after all this. I will push these thoughts over to him, with my mind. Hoping the process of osmosis will feed them into his brain.

"I… I…" Damn, he is stalling over his words. "I did not know I would have to do that. You have to believe me, Hugo. I only became aware of the situation when we got there."

"Shit, Femi. That makes me an accomplice." My pulse quickens and I feel dizzy. When I am aware of impending doom and fear kicking in, this is the feeling I get. I jump to the worst-case scenario. It's the extreme, no in-between. But in this situation, this is justified; there is no halfway house here.

"No, Hugo. You were not actually there, were you?"

"Who the hell has been carrying it with you? Who the hell has been making sure it is secure while we have been travelling?" I spit my words out. My mouth is dry and my lips want to split open with the heat and dehydration. I throw my hand up and point at the package. My hand trembles. I am not sure if it is shaking due to the turbulence or because of my inner rage and fear. "Look, it's fucking sitting right there between us. I am here. Fuck, this is so fucked."

"Hugo, please calm down."

Poor choice of words, Femi.

"How the hell do you want me to calm down? I have helped you steal one of the world's, sorry, I mean, *the* world's most powerful artefacts, which was believed as destroyed many years ago. There is a clear reason for me not to be calm right now."

I can tell Femi is lost for words and he does seem concerned at my reaction, which gives me hope. Gives me hope that he is on the good side.

"And who are these Germans you mentioned? Are they who you stole it from? Are they after us? Are they the ones who followed us in the bush? Femi, please, I deserve to know."

"I will. I promise I will tell you what I know. But not here." He nods over in the direction of the driver's cabin. "Once we get dropped off, we'll get some food in us. It will help us think straighter when we speak. I promise, Hugo. All will work out fine."

How many times have I heard those words in my life? Nothing ever works out 'fine'. The landscape is changing around us as we drive. It's becoming more built up. More clusters of buildings that look inhabited. Fences and motorbikes dotted around. The odd person walking around in the heat. I look over to the package. What a fucking mess I am in.

21

Before

I step out onto Davis Street after the session with Fiona, not before gathering my thoughts and making sure I can keep it together with Femi whom I am meeting now. It is a grey and dull day, just how I prefer the weather. Perhaps reflective of my mood and emotions. But I tend to think better when there is less sun out. I am not sure what Femi and I will work on today. He was not that specific when we last met about what he wanted to discuss. I suppose that he reports back to his boss each day, like a mission report back to base. The fact that he has now seen the photograph of the painting being in circulation around 1970, he has enough to go on and trust that my work stands up to the mark. The photograph has both the first set of *Sunflowers* present that van Gogh painted, side by side. Although both of them have not been seen in public for many years, it has been assumed as fact that one of the *Sunflowers* was purchased around 1908 by a private Japanese collector. This is of the beautiful sunflower with a turquoise background, with the code F453 in the art world. This painting is believed to be held by a private collector whereas the second painting, the emotional deep royal blue background one, code F459, is the one that was purchased in 1921 and was destroyed in the Japanese bombings of World War Two. But, the picture I have explains a different narrative to that story.

Do I walk or get a taxi over to Covent Garden? Walking will help get my mind off the session and let the interaction with the hustle and bustle of London prepare my thoughts for Femi. I will walk; I better message him to explain I will be late. He would already be expecting that in any case, as I do not think I have once yet been on time for any of our meeting arrangements.

'On way, sorry, got delayed, as always. PS it's not a hangover. See you soon.'

Instant reply from him, 'OK.'

As always, short and to the point – not sure how to take that – is it an 'OK' in the sense that he is fine with it or an 'OK' in the manner of 'you fucking retard, always late and nothing ever is going to change with you'? I may have just gone from one extreme to the other.

I know the exact route I want to take to get to Covent Garden. It will be down Oxford Street towards the intersection with Tottenham Court Road and then I need to take a right down Dean Street to take me through Soho and into Chinatown, bringing me right outside Leicester Square tube station. Covent Garden is just round the corner from there. It's a route that I do regularly to get my mind lost amongst all the other thoughts floating in this city.

I have faced some of my fears when it comes to Covent Garden. It was a place I always felt safe in. It was my personal playground to feed off all the energy. Then came that day when she decided to rip that safety away from me. That day she chose to devalue me in public. That day her audience was everyone around us, watching as they walked past in the arches section of the square. We stood outside the restaurant called Buns&Buns, which we once had lunch in where she stripped every aspect of my existence and walked off with her friend, feeling very victorious. But I have settled my demons with that place now and no longer does that memory inflict chaos within me.

I feel a buzz in my pocket from my phone. The text from Femi reads, 'Whereabouts is good to meet for you in Covent Garden?'

'Let's meet outside Buns&Buns restaurant. It's in the arches market bit,' I smile as I reply.

I spot Femi leaning against the wall as I approach the restaurant. He is wearing a black baseball cap and reading some sort of newspaper.

"Sorry, man. I have no idea how time got away with me today." I feel I need to apologise to Femi for my lack of timekeeping. I do not want him to think I am not committed to this project, especially as I am getting paid for my time.

"Don't worry, today we are just hanging out. It is our day off."

This has taken me by surprise. A day off? If it *is* a day off, why would Femi still want to meet me? Why not just say that earlier in the day so we could do our own thing?

"Day off. What does that mean exactly?"

Femi folds his newspaper away and places it under his arm.

"Well, after reporting all the findings to my boss, they have confirmed that the information you have provided confirms the most convincing evidence they suspected."

I waited for Femi to finish his sentence. He was looking around as he spoke, which made me look around like we were both looking for someone or waiting for someone else. He looked back at me after being satisfied with scanning the area.

"Well, your research confirms their assumptions that the painting they have located is perhaps the same one that is present in your photograph, so, now, the next step is to go to the painting and get up close and personal with it so you can do your magic."

"And where is that, exactly? I mean, where do we have to travel to?"

Just a smile back from Femi and I understood that it indicated he did not want to tell me that at present.

"So, this place any good to eat?" Femi poked his finger at the restaurant opposite us with his rolled-up newspaper. 'Buns&Buns'. Typical, it's like he read my mind to go down memory lane.

"It's average, but a good place to start."

It's not too busy as we find a table to sit, towards the back of the restaurant. It has floor to ceiling glass windows all around. It is actually an encased place inside the arches aspect of Covent Garden's square. Like a fancy exclusive portacabin. As the name implies, the menu consists of various fillings in a bun. I study Femi as he rolls his eyes up and down the list.

"Not much of a great selection on the menu," Femi says, while putting the menu down and looking to the tables around us to see what others are eating.

"We can go somewhere else if you prefer."

"No, no, let's have a light bite here and then we can

always get something later to eat."

So, Femi does intend on spending the whole day and evening with me. This feels like us hanging out, as friends, but with a caveat. I really don't have a choice because I am getting paid for my time. That makes me feel like a male companion. OK, shake that thought out of my head. Actually, could Femi be attracted to me? No – fuck! Get that out of my head too.

We both decide on the lobster filled buns and a side salad with sweet potato fries.

"So, Hugo, tell me, what is that book you keep with you every time we have met?"

Femi starts the topic of conversation as we wait for our food. At first I am confused about what he means, then I understand that he has noticed my reading book that I have with me every time I leave home. It is lying on the table, next to my glass full of water.

"Oh this, it's just a book I am reading at the moment. I always make sure I have a book on the go. I suppose it serves a couple of purposes for me."

Femi reaches over to the book and flips it over to see the front.

"*Love in the time of Cholera*. Umm, interesting title for a book. Let me guess, a tragic love story when both lovers die from contracting cholera?"

I suddenly feel myself becoming overprotective of the book and take it from Femi's grip.

"Actually, yes, a love story, but very poetic in its nature. It highlights the importance of endurance and true inner resilience when it comes to real love."

Femi takes his baseball cap off and lets it rest on his lap. His expression is soft.

"Tell me. You seem like a true romantic at heart…" He pauses. I am waiting for him to finish what he was going to ask, but he just sits there and takes a sip of water.

"Romance is an art that I have yet not only to master but also to understand what it truly entails for me."

"Here you go, guys." Our food has arrived just in time as I wasn't really wanting to have a conversation about the uncomfortable aspects of my pathetic attempts at having relationships.

"So, tell me about you. I mean, I know nothing much at all about *your* life. Do you have a family back home in Zimbabwe?"

Femi leans back in his chair after taking a bite from his bun. He took his time chewing the food and I could tell from his eyes that he was using this time to understand what areas of my question to tackle and answer. This always indicates some element of being uncomfortable with what the truth is.

"My village is situated just over 50 miles west of one of the bigger cities in Zimbabwe." He continues to chew his food.

"Which city?" I ask like I know anything about the geography of Zimbabwe.

"Bulawayo."

"Oh, OK." My answer.

Femi chuckles after he has emptied his mouthful and swallowed his food.

"What do you mean, 'oh, OK' like you know where that city is?"

"Hey, don't be so narrow-minded. What makes you think a pale guy like me is not well travelled?" I stare back at Femi with a serious look. But it doesn't last and I laugh.

"Yeh, you are right, I have no fucking clue where that is."

"Well, it's a beautiful part of the world. The village is surrounded by so many fresh smells and sounds and sights of real Mother Earth. It was always such a blessing to wake up in the morning to the feeling of just real earth."

I look down at our food sitting on the table hearing Femi's words and think this must be such a step down for him with how food looks and tastes. I think he read my mind with my thoughts.

"The food always tasted so distinctive for each of the various ingredients we had. I mean, you could feel the taste buds on your tongue dancing to each taste. Everything came from the soil or from the trees. The local rivers provided us with the lightest fish that we would steam or grill depending on the time of year."

"It sounds so healthy. No wonder you have that strong look to you." I just heard my own words back at me and they came out so gay. "I mean, natural foods are always good for the body, not like all these modern-day foods." I feel myself rambling now. "Even all the organic, free-range and eco-friendly stuff is not really up to the mark."

"Well, Hugo, at least such cities, like London, will always have a supply of food. Yes, I would agree with you, this food here is… well, isn't what I would call 'real food', but the supply chain keeps people in cities like this fed. There is always an alternative to get here. But back home, the supply is always dependent on the seasons. It only takes a couple of months of not great weather to really knock things out for us back home."

I am so tempted to ask about his facial scar. I can feel myself conscious not to focus on it as we speak. I look everywhere else but directly at the scar, but it keeps drawing me in to notice it. I am sure he would tell me if he wanted to.

"When was the last time you visited home?"

Femi's eyes drop as I ask this. His shoulders drop too and it seems he has shrunk in size sitting there suddenly.

He lets out a sigh.

"Its been too long, Hugo. Too long."

He takes another bite of his bun and I can sense that this is the end of the conversation for him.

"So, Hugo." Bits of crumbs fall out of his mouth as he speaks. "Tonight you are going to show me some sights of London. I want to experience some of the real highlights of this city, as we have the day off."

I smile at him and I feel comfortable having a friend today. This feels nice, this feels safe, this feels normal. Perhaps this is what I need more of, just having no expectations, no concerns about hidden agendas, no needing to please anyone, no need to think they want something else from me. Yes, this is what normality feels like.

"Well, Femi, let's see where the night takes us."

22

Before

How the hell did I sleep with the blinds open last night? Light never lets me sleep. I must have been so out of it. 10.36 AM showing on the phone. Not bad. At least it's before noon. A couple of texts. It is always nice to feel that I have people messaging me. The majority of the time, I get disappointed that it's one of the marketing companies. I remember the days when I used to stare at the phone for hours and hours on end, willing her to message me. Trying to will her with my mind to use her fingers to type a message. I got to the point when even if the message was a demeaning one, at least it would have some form of communication. But it never happened. Eventually, the time between me fixating and becoming obsessed with the screen would become longer and longer and I would only check the screen now and again. Days passed into weeks and weeks and then into months and I understood – it was over. Why would it not be? I was a shit. Well, I think I was anyway. But according to Fiona, who also became my relationship counsellor throughout that period, I was projecting all my inner issues into the relationship because I had not understood what had occurred to me all those years ago. Even to this day, I try to read into every word of her last communication to me. It was on Christmas Eve and it was, 'Merry Christmas'. I mean, how much more is there to analyse into that message? Yet I wanted a hidden hope in it. I obviously had to reply with an essay of a text back. Just a dick of a move. No wonder there was no reply from my New Year's wishes message to her. And that was it. Silence since.

I can hear the dogs barking away next door. The owners, my neighbours, whom I have not met after all these years, always yell at the dogs when they bark in that manner. It is like they actually hate the dogs. The screen of my phone lights up again. I reach over and unlock the screen – three text messages all from Femi. I open them in the order they were received.

'Great night, Hugo. Loved the Scarfes Bar. See you tomorrow' received at 01.25 AM.

'Hugo, don't tell me you are hungover. It was only a couple of drinks! Message me when you get this,' received at 09.27 AM.

'Get up and call me. We have to get things in place for our travels,' received at 10.42 AM.

I throw the phone onto the bed, close my eyes and roll over onto the cold side of the pillow. I have never worked out why the best sleep occurs when it's time to get up in the morning. But I am sure I could sleep for another couple of hours, but all that comes to mind is Femi's steaming eyes and that stare when he is not impressed. Time for a shower.

'Managed to recover and drag yourself out of bed, did you?'

Sarcastic comments from Femi never truly sound sarcastic. They always sound like meaningful accusations and make me want to defend myself. He did not wait for me to order his breakfast or lunch or whatever time it is at the moment for food. I just managed to have a glass of water as I rushed out this morning. Does he never get cold? He is wearing a t-shirt, it's probably not even ten degrees at the moment and he is sitting outside at this French café.

"Hey, come on. Give me some credit. We had a good night last night. It was worth the lie-in."

I pull out the chair opposite him and take a seat. There is a checked blanket on the back of the chair and I am tempted to put it over my knees, but I know Femi would lose some manly respect for me if I did that. He is rolling around some fried tomatoes and sausages on his plate. I can see the grease pool around the plate and my stomach does a little jump inside. I don't think I am hungry after all. How many Negronis did I have last night?

"I never asked. I should have asked before, but you have a passport that is valid, right?" Femi does not look up at me as he speaks.

The waiter comes out once he spots me sitting opposite Femi.

"Good afternoon, would you like some food?"

I look at the plate sitting in front of Femi again and decide that my stomach needs something gentle.

"Do you do a fruit salad, please, a cappuccino and a bottle of still water?" He nods and walks off inside.

"Yes, I am sure it is in date and valid." I mentally try and go through my apartment where the passport would be hiding. I think the last time I used it was to go to France, on the Eurostar, with her. That was ages ago. I have not seen it since. Crap, I hope it is in the apartment somewhere. "Why, are we travelling?"

Femi takes a forkful of his food and pushes the plate to the side, using a napkin to clean the corner of his mouth.

"I think we have done enough in London with you and we are satisfied that you will be able to appraise the painting on location now."

"Well, that's good news. So, where and when are we going?" My dry looking fruit salad arrives. It's placed in front of me with a smile from the staff.

Snippets of last night are coming back to me now and I recall how it was an evening of just speaking about anything and everything apart from work aspects. I recall that not once did I feel uncomfortable or did I fixate on hidden agendas from Femi. I actually took the evening for what it was. Two friends, out and about just having a good time. No wonder I perhaps slept well last night. Either that or the alcohol. Well, a combination of the two, I think.

As Femi brings the endless movement of his mouthful of food to an end, he explains the next stage of this.

"So, the painting is in Egypt. In Luxor, to be precise."

That has taken me by surprise. I thought we would be travelling to Europe somewhere, perhaps the Netherlands or France. But Egypt? Fuck, the sun and the heat.

"So, we will need to visit the family who are guardians of the painting on site there in Luxor as obviously it will be too difficult to arrange the logistics to have the painting transported elsewhere."

From Femi's facial expression, I can tell that he has more to say, that perhaps this is not as straightforward as it all sounds. But he hesitates.

"So, I will need a visa, right?" This was the only thing that came to mind to ask right now. I did not want to push Femi about what else he wants to say, just in case he feels I am not ready to hear it.

"Do not worry about that. We can take care of that quickly; we just need to have your passport so I can arrange that. It will take less than 48 hours."

Another question that comes to mind and this is something that will play a major part is that I have no idea who is going to pay for my travel, stay and expenses. I know I am getting paid for my time, but if I am expected to pay for the travel costs and wherever we are staying, I don't think I have anything in reserve to pay for that, at present.

"Before you get your mind all racing with thoughts, as I know how you can be, Hugo, the flight costs and where we will be staying will all be part of your expenses and so you will not have to worry about that."

How the fuck does he do that? Like, read my mind all the time.

I build up the courage to ask some burning questions after taking a sip of my cappuccino. I totally forgot to ask for oat milk and I know that my stomach will pay the price for that later. Oat milk is another good thing she introduced to me to help me with my IBS. I smile every time I say the words 'with oat milk, please'. It makes me feel so empowered. Thanks to her.

"The family that has the painting... Am I allowed to know anything more about them? Like, have they always had it? And how have they kept it so hidden all these years?"

I watch Femi's reaction to my questions. He takes a

deep sigh before replying.

"Hugo, even some facts I have not been made aware of. I do not even know the full details of the location as yet. All I know is that we need to get all our bits ready for travel to Luxor."

I study Femi's face in great detail as he says this and I believe him. I suppose, due to the potential discovery of this painting, everything will be on a need-to-know basis and very top-secret and confidential in nature.

"OK, sure. So, what's next then? You will need the passport, I assume." I have not suggested this before, but I now trust Femi. "Why don't you come to my apartment with me to pick the passport up?"

Femi gazes at me. His head tilts slightly to the side. He opens his mouth to say something and then thinks better of it and closes it again. I try not to focus on the scar on his face, but it's difficult not to in the daylight. I am sure I didn't ask about it last night, although it would have been the perfect time to ask as there was alcohol in both of our systems, so inhibitions would have been lower.

"I won't need it today. It is too late to get the visa organised today, in any case. Remember to keep it with you next time we meet and you can give it to me then. Tomorrow." He then leans onto the table, closer to me. "Tomorrow morning." He lingers on the word 'morning'.

"I got the message loud and clear, boss. Be on time."

"Good, now that we have that sorted we should put a shopping list together of things we will need to take with us to Egypt."

I can't help but feel a sense of nostalgia. Two friends planning a trip together.

"Have you finished with that?" Out of nowhere, the

staff member returns, standing over my shoulder. I am not sure who he is speaking to but Femi is first to respond.

"Yes, thank you. I was not as hungry as I had thought and it was very filling." He picks the plate up with its grease rolling around on the surface and hands it over to the waiter. My fruit salad is untouched at present and I feel guilty that I now do not want it, but do not dare to say so. I motion to pick a slice of dry apple from the plate to show I am interested in the food. It worked as he takes Femi's plate and lets us be.

"So, what kind of items do you think we need to take with us?" I was thinking of paperwork related items like various forms of research from me, papers, reference articles or items needed to verify the artwork. Perhaps sampling materials, ways to record the data we discover and so on.

"Have you ever been to Egypt before, Hugo?" Obviously, Femi knows the answer to that as I could tell by his tone that he very well knows I have not travelled to the continent of Africa in the past.

"Nope."

"Well, it will be hot. I mean, hot and humid and dry. So make sure you have the appropriate clothing for that. Also, we need to pack light as we may need to travel a bit to various sites, depending on the location of the painting."

"What do you mean 'location of the painting'?" I ask, with a confused look on my face.

"Yes. The family may be moving it from one location to another due to…"

He cuts off mid-sentence.

"Due to what, Femi?"

"Well, remember I said that the painting may be on

the move soon, hence the need for us to travel soon before *it* does. Well, the reason for that is due to security aspects to keep the painting in safe locations from time to time."

I ponder the words that he has just said. It makes sense on the face of them, but something seems unsettled about this whole aspect. But, who am I to question? My remit is to have provided details of my research, which I have done, and now to help aid in the task of studying the painting up close and personal and to give my opinion, as professional as I can, on the authenticity of the painting.

Femi continues, "So, you need appropriate footwear for trekking and we will need bags, no bigger than hand luggage size, for all our belongings."

This seems like a camping expedition now. Femi's wrist watch catches my attention. I saw it before but now I get a good look at it in the daylight it looks like a fancy military grade watch. Very expensive and fancy.

"Yes, sure, Femi; I am sure I have understood what kind of things I need to take."

Femi smiles and nods, giving a sense of understanding. I smile back and glance at the watch again and make a mental note to order one from Amazon for the trip. I want to be part of the club.

23

Now

I do not know anymore what is making my head spin. Is it the heat of the sun bearing down on me or is it the heat from being an accomplice with this guy, whom I trusted as my friend with stealing the most valuable works of art that may ever be present in this world?

We both, in silence, disembark from the back of the truck. There is no conversation as we are left with our thoughts. I naturally take the bags, which leaves Femi to carry the package on his back again. He will be damned if he thinks I will carry it anymore. The less contact I have with it in the open now, the better. In fact, it is becoming more and more appealing that I make a run for it with my passport, get on the first plane back to London and report all this to someone. As I run that play through my head, it becomes evident that it is no longer an option. I know too much. I am a target out here and likely will remain a target back in London if I run now.

The securing of the package on Femi's back is now done with a much swifter pace. Primarily because we are out in the open and secondarily, because I just need to get this over and done with now, whatever it is.

As the driver comes round to make sure all is OK with

us, he told us that we are south of central Cairo, in the Islamic sector of Cairo.

"Thank you so much. You have been very kind to us." Femi does all the speaking.

The driver bids us farewell and drives off in a trail of sand from the truck tyres.

I can see why this city is one of the most densely populated cities in the world. It seems we are just on the outskirts of the main streets of this sector, but even so, there is a real sense of urgency with everything here. I can see in all directions; alleyways and bazaars that take me back to scenes from *One Thousand and One Nights*, the collection of Middle Eastern folk tales.

I move over to the side of a building to get some shade over me, placing the bags down on the floor beside me as I do so.

"Water, water, sir?"

A young lad approaches out of nowhere and pushes a small water bottle at me. He must be no more than ten or 11 years of age. Over his shoulder he carries an open bag with a number of small bottles of water. I can see how worn his hands are and there is dirt under every fingernail. Looking into his eyes, he has an obvious kindness to him.

"No, no; I am fine, thank you." The child continues to stand there in front of me, holding the small bottle of water out at me. I feel a sense of guilt saying this to him, but I still have no local currency on me. Why would I? I would have had but Femi takes care of everything. This is probably the most extreme co-dependency situation I am in out here.

"Go now, boy. We do not need to be bothered." Femi walks over eventually and sternly warns the child off who sulks off saying something under his breath and kicking up some sand with his heels.

"That was a bit harsh. Then again, I don't think I should be surprised with anything from the real Femi I am know now."

He ignores me, pulls his phone out and checks a couple of messages I assume, and then swipes it shut.

"It is not far to where we are meeting the curator. We will need to walk through the Khan el-Khalili bazaar area."

He takes the lead, crosses the street and walks off. I watch him stride off, confident and standing tall as always. I stay where I am, in the shade with our bags by my side.

The narrow thoroughfare is busy with people weaving in and out and carts pulled by donkeys. Everyone seems to be concentrating on getting to a destination or on selling something to passers-by. Femi stands out with his build. He finally looks back over to check on me and locks eyes with me.

We stand there, watching each other, waiting for the other to make the first move. Like a Western showdown. All I keep thinking is how betrayed I feel, especially how he seemed so different in London. He seemed genuinely interested in me in London. As unconditional friends would be. But it was all a fucking lie. I see him shake his head at me as he succumbs to the fact that I will not move. He reluctantly walks back over to me.

"Hugo, you can't stay out here, alone."

"Let me fucking guess. It's not safe for me because people are looking for us. Maybe it's not safe because you bloody stole that thing on your back."

"Hugo, there is so much more to this than you realise, and, yes, it will be difficult to explain everything to you, but once we meet with the curator and you get the inspection done, we can get you back to London."

"When did you know?"

Femi looks agitated at my question.

"Know what?"

Is he really trying to piss me off to the maximum now?

"Did you know when I met you in London all that time ago that it was going to turn out like this?"

I sound like a wounded ex that has just found out he is cheating on me. Takes me back to one of the precursors to when she thought I was cheating on her when she found a message on my phone. Simple message from a female friend thanking me for coffee and saying that we should do it again soon and that Rome will be amazing, it's beautiful there. But that was misinterpreted in a way that I was sleeping with this person and I would be taking this person to Rome with me. Well, that resulted with a slap around the face for me and a hole in the wall in the bedroom from her slamming the door. How I still blame myself over that, not because I *was* sleeping with anyone else and not because I was going to Rome with anyone else; in fact, I wanted to take *her* to Rome over Christmas, but I knew she wanted to spend time with her family. But, I am still upset because that was the moment of no return for both of us. We both knew that night, deep down, that there was no turning back within our own minds and hearts.

"Hugo. Even I have been made to do things that I was unaware of when I first took this role. I have a lot to lose. You won't understand..." His voice trails off with a sense of fear and disappointment in his voice.

I can see another couple of kids gathering from the corner of my vision, ready to sell me something.

The traffic keeps moving at pace in front of us both, but I am determined not to move an inch before Femi tells me more about all of this.

"Try me, Femi. Because right now, it seems I also have a lot to lose with this as prison does not seem like a very attractive option for me, at present."

"Let's not do this here, please."

There is a look of concern in his eyes. He does seem genuinely concerned about something. I recall his words that he was 'made to do things' that he was not made aware of. Could it be that he is also now in the same situation as me? That of being betrayed and let down? Is that why he perhaps has this sense of empathy towards me at the moment?

"Where is your family, Femi?"

His eyes widen at my sentence. The whole stature of his body alters in those moments. Shoulders rise and contract in a tense motion. Even with the package on his back, which, until now, he carried with such ease, appears as if it weighs a couple of tons. We are still standing in the shade and yet, now, I see the formation of tiny sweat beads across his forehead. By his side, his hands are clenched into tight balls of fury or fear, I can't work out which right now.

He opens his mouth to say something, yet no words come out. I am sure I just saw his bottom lip tremble slightly. His family – this seems to have his family involved.

"Femi, what is it?"

"We need to go, now." He turns and walks back in the direction that we just came from, weaving through the people in the street. Fuck this, I need to know what is going on and get my arse back to London, but it seems the only way that is going to happen is to get this appraisal over and done with and get on a flight.

Femi is back to his normal stride pattern, making easy work of the distance to cover wherever we are going to now. I can sense I rattled him with the question about his family as not a word has been said since.

The streets are back-to-back busy now. Bodies bustling and moving all over the place.

"These are the medieval stone gates to the entrance to the bazaar. It will be even more crowded in there, so let's try and stay close together." Femi points a hand up to the huge stone structure ahead of us that has a high domed passageway leading through the carved stone.

As we walk through the gateway, it opens up to splendours of visual and aromatic delights. The rainbow of colours all around make my eyes jump with delight. I see fabrics of all manner of materials, from clothes to rugs to textile wall coverings. Light reflects the mountains of copper and brass ornaments piled up in some of the open shop front carts. The fruit sellers are busy refilling the displays of mangos, oranges and bananas on their overflowing cart stalls. The smell infiltrates the air around me with exotic spices and other various pungent scents.

I stay close behind Femi as he leads us through the maze. Off the main path there seems to be a maze of narrow, canvas-covered alleyways crammed with even more shops selling goods of various forms. Interspersed between the locals, hordes of tourists stand out, just like me, I assume. I catch the odd bit of eye contact from fellow non-natives and give a nervous smile or nod of appreciation that we are the common outsiders.

"This way." Femi takes a sharp right into one of the alleyways. It is less busy than others and has fewer carts selling goods. The paving is more uneven and cobbled down this alleyway and the walls on either side seem to be in need of repair. More debris, cracks and weeds than the Main Street we just came from. The beaten and worn out wooden doors with peeling paint tell me that there must be residential buildings down this passage.

"Are we going to the curator's house?" I ask, after looking back to check there was no one following or local to overhear us.

Again, slight hesitation from Femi before he replies. He stops and turns back to face me.

"Hugo, I told you I would protect and look after you. Please remember that."

"What is that supposed to mean? Where are we going?" Fuck, this is not good. I have a horrible feeling inside me rising like a volcano. My insides are shaking and I feel I want to vomit but with nothing but burning bile and acid from my guts.

"You will have your protected time with the painting soon and this ordeal will be all over." Femi turns and walks up to a door that I had not noticed until just now. There is an iron gate covering the doorway with a wooden door behind it. This door seems well maintained and very secure compared to all the others we have passed. He rattles the knocker high on the door and waits for it to be answered.

24

Before

I always get this extra excitement when it comes to the airport. This is only something that has recently occurred. When I say recently, I would say in the last three or so years. Prior to this, the anxiety of people at the airport with its busy nature would put me into such a frenzy that I recall once I was unable to get on a flight as I could not stand in line to check in. It was all too overwhelming for me. I remember the heat encompassing every aspect of my body at that time. The sweat beads starting to form on my forehead. The intense shaky feeling from within me, causing the heart to race and resonate in my ears. I can recall how the rush of blood would drum against my eardrums along with the feelings of nausea and dizzy spells. It was a particular visit to Gatwick Airport. The destination was Rome, I am sure of it. Was I alone or with someone? That bit is a blank at present, but in any case, I didn't get on the flight and decided to alight the first flight the next morning instead so I could plan getting to the check-in queue before anyone else. I stayed in the hotel overnight, the Hilton on-site at Gatwick. What a stupid waste of money.

But here I am now, or shall I say, here *we* are, Femi

and I, at Heathrow Airport, London. Actually, strictly speaking, London only has one airport and that is City Airport, not Heathrow or Gatwick. Our flight departs at 2.35 PM and lands in Luxor at local time 9.40 PM. It's a five-hour flight, non-stop. I can tolerate a four-hour flight, just about. I am sure the extra hour will be fine. I have no idea how Femi will fit in economy, but I was dreaming that we would fly business or first class.

We have two hours before the gates open. Femi wanted to get here in plenty of time just in case of traffic on the way. I do feel much calmer being in airports at present, with all the work I have done with Fiona on such spaces. I think getting me on the London Underground tube was the major step. If I could be comfortable in that environment, which is much more dense and compact around people, then airports comparatively give a much more open environment. We only have one bag each, classed as hand luggage, so this should make things much smoother at the other end in Luxor.

"So, we have loads of time." I make conversation with Femi as we pass security and get into the duty-free area of the departures lounge. We have not spoken much at all today on the way here in the taxi about the work to be done in Luxor.

"What's the time now?"

I take this proud moment to flash my new purchase, the watch on my wrist for this trip. "It's 12.24."

We walk slowly pass the alcohol and perfume counters dotted around us. Femi is not taking any interest in them at all.

"Let's get some food."

This was a welcome suggestion from Femi as my stomach

was doing flips and I am sure the security personnel back there could hear the growling and had raised an eyebrow or two.

"Sounds good to me."

Apart from the bare, simple facts of our destination of Luxor, there is not much more I know about the actual itinerary of what happens when we land. I am hoping Femi will start explaining some of these aspects now, over some food.

As we browse around, the normal airport food places range from the quick sandwich venues to full English pub styles. I am glad when Femi does not spend too much time glancing over the quick sandwich places.

"How about this place?" Femi stops at one called Pilots Bar & Kitchen. He scans the menu that is on a stand at the entrance. I look inside and it seems like it has a gastro-pub feel to it. I don't bother looking at the menu with Femi; I could eat anything.

"Looks good to me. Let's get a table."

I can sense that Femi will expect me to start the questions related to Luxor. I think he has not explained anything on purpose to make the relevant questions flow and so he can provide only what I need, to feel reassured. As we wait for our lunch, me the battered traditional fish and chips and Femi the classic hamburger and fries, I get all the questions formulated in my head.

Femi chose to sit on the wooden chair while I slid into the booth. Every time Femi moved, I could hear the chair creak and it was only a matter of time until the spokes fell out of the back of the chair with his weight.

"So, tell me more about this place we are going to in Luxor. You mentioned the painting was being looked after by someone and was going to be on the move again soon."

Femi pours us water from the jug on the table. The ice cubes fall into my glass as he pours and causes the water to splash over the table.

"We will be meeting a family there. The family have been in possession of the painting for many years now." That was all he said and then he looked around in anticipation of the food. I was hoping he would continue without me prompting, but when we spoke next it was totally off subject. "You sure you have everything you need for the trip?" He looked down at my hand luggage bag resting by my side.

"Of course. Why are you worried? I just followed the basic rules you explained about the trip. 'Pack light, it will be hot, need robust footwear'."

"Yes, I know, Hugo, but I was hoping you would have spent an afternoon with me just going through what you were intending to pack."

A feeling of discontent has suddenly come over me. Femi obviously feels I am incompetent in packing for a trip or following simple instructions.

"If you would like, I could unpack all the contents here, on the table, and you can approve or discard what you feel." My tone was very much sarcastic in nature and he picked up on this.

"Oh, Hugo, you are having your hormones jumping all over at the moment. I was just asking, that's all, in a manner to make the trip as easy and comfortable for you as possible."

"Well, it's fine. I am sure I packed appropriately." I still have not forgotten my initial track of conversation and want to get back to that. The food arrives and I decide to wait until a couple of food bites are in us before tackling the subject again.

The battered fish seemed like a good idea at the time, but it is a very much to be desired taste. More batter than fish. The oily taste reminds me that I will have to get some Buscopan from a pharmacy before we get on the plane. Knowing my luck, my IBS will play up mid-flight and I hate using toilets on plane journeys. There is always that nervousness that someone is waiting outside the door to come in next and they will have noted every sound and movement that occurred in there.

"So, the painting. Is it in a museum, in a private collection… where and with whom?"

Femi puts down his burger after taking a decent sized bite from it. He chews slowly, but with purpose.

"Well, it's not in a museum, is it, Hugo, otherwise we would not have had any need for you to be on this trip, would we."

I have decided that sarcasm does not suit Femi at all. I will make a mental note to tell him at some stage. I do not respond to his comment and let him get the message that I want something more substantial.

He lets out his customary sigh and leans back, using the napkin to wipe the corner of his mouth and fingers from all the grease and sauce from the burger.

"The painting is part of a private collection and has been in the same family for many years, according to what I have been told." Femi impressed on that last sentence to make it clear that this information is what he has been told and not information that he has discovered or, indeed, known as fact.

"So, why do they, or your boss, want me to appraise

the painting? Surely there are so many other better placed people around the world to do such a job."

"Well, Hugo, I am sure you now understand the, shall we say, sensitive nature of such a discovery. So the knowledge of it being real and authenticated needs to be as covert as possible."

It was interesting to hear the choice of words that Femi used. 'Covert' – this was increasingly having the flavour of a mission rather than an appraisal of artwork.

Femi continued, "There is already concern that there is some unwanted attention to the family that holds the painting, which is why we are required to go now before it is moved again, for security reasons."

"When you say security reasons, what exactly do you mean by that?" I ask while attempting to regain some interest in my food, however unappealing it now seems. I am sure I can get some of the actual fish out from the casing of batter that surrounds it.

"I have a feeling you are worried about your security. Is that the case, Hugo?" There is a slight smile on his face as he asks me.

"Well, I would like to know that I will be safe and make it back home in once piece. Of course, I am slightly worried about the security aspects, but I was more asking about the security of the painting you are referring to as you keep mentioning that it may be on the move again soon."

Femi pushed his body forward onto the table again and looked at his food, the remainder of the burger that gradually seemed to be falling apart.

"I don't know too many details on that front, but yes, I have been told that the family may want the painting moved at some point and, obviously, we will not be privy to the new location. So this is our only shot at this."

Femi's logic seems sound. What is abundantly clear from all this is that whomever Femi is working for, his boss, or whomever it is, seems very well connected and powerful, with resources and extensive reach.

I am still pushing the food around my plate with my fork. I can sense Femi looking from my plate to my face.

"Is something troubling you, Hugo?"

What a question. My initial response would be the honest,

"Yes, Femi, there are a shitload of things troubling me. Where would you like me to start and how long have we got?" But I decide to be polite.

"The food here is crap." My response makes Femi laugh.

"I thought it was just my burger."

25

Before

"Wait, Hugo; the seatbelt sign is still on."

Femi looks over to me as I desperately try to unbuckle my seatbelt as the plane touches down in Luxor. I was hoping that I would get the aisle seat but, obviously, Femi and his long limbs took precedence to sit in that seat and I got the window seat. Not one for looking out through the window for five hours, my legs are aching from not being able to stretch them all this time.

"It's not like we are going to really crash now, are we, on the tarmac?" I comment as he rolls his eyes at me. "Fine; be like all the other typical tourists on the plane and jump up to try and get your bag before everyone else. But you *do* know we will only get off the plane in order, right?"

My ears pop again and I honestly don't care what Femi says. I managed to finish my book on the journey and realised that I do not have another one on standby yet. But I'm hoping that this trip will be so action-packed that I won't be left to my own devices for too long.

The night is dark outside and as we descended I could see the scattered lights of outbuildings, then gradually the density of the buildings and then the lights increasing as we got closer to the airport and the centre of Luxor.

I look at my watch as the plane slowly taxis in to its allocated slot at the terminal. It is still set to UK time. I am sure Femi's super fancy watch automatically sets the time to the local one. I will deal with mine when we get to the hotel room, wherever and whenever that will be.

I look around me and I can see most people now standing in the aisle and starting to reach for the overhead areas to get their hand luggage.

"Yeh, looks like everyone is going to listen to the likes of you, Femi. Come on, I need to stretch my legs; they are aching from sitting here in the corner while you got the leg room, man."

The rush of humid air hits my face as we walk off the plane and to the terminal via the adjoining makeshift tunnel. I sat mostly under the air conditioning cold stream on the flight to keep me cool, but the sharp contrast in temperature is slightly more extreme than I had imagined.

The flight was only about three-quarters full, so we breezed through security and immigration. It was comforting to know a return flight was booked for next Tuesday. This reassured me of the fact that I will not be stuck out here. Femi was not booked on the flight back as he had said he would be flying elsewhere from here when we are done.

There was no need to wait for any further luggage as we had our two carry-on bags anyway. Femi led the way to the exit of the terminal. It was much busier outside than I had anticipated at this late hour. The lay-by directly outside the exit had a line of minicabs lined up with the drivers standing outside, hustling for a fare. There did not seem to be any order to how the passengers chose a minicab. It was more a fact of who shouted the most.

"Wait over here, Hugo. I will find us transport." Femi pointed to a spot under a lamp-post over to the far end of the lay-by. He handed his bag to me. I am glad I wore a loose, baggy t-shirt now as I can already feel it starting to stick to my back and arms. As I look up at the lamp, the glow shining down on me, I can see all the flies buzzing around the glow. They must be mosquitoes. Femi did reassure me that no extra precautions were needed for aspects of infectious diseases here. He did suggest to check my hepatitis B and tetanus immunisations were up to date, however, which I checked and they were. I questioned about getting a yellow fever immunisation because I had read somewhere that certain parts of the Nile may be at risk, but Femi said there was no need. I was not sure why at the time I took his word for it, but he seemed confident in his stance and so I did not seem to think anything else of it.

Looking around I see most people leaving the airport seem to be residents returning to Luxor. They all appear to be sure of where they were headed and confident who to avoid out of the minicab drivers, water sellers and others hanging around the terminal. It seemed that the muppets like me are the prey for all these street vendors. I watch Femi in the distance as he chooses a guy leaning causally on his minicab and then talks to him. The guy seems so at ease and relaxed with a cigarette hanging from his mouth. I can make out the guy nodding and Femi shaking his head and then another few exchanges taking place and then Femi seems to nod in agreement. It seems they are laughing now, which I assume is always a good sign.

Femi walks back over to me. His long strides make easy work of the distance between us.

"We have a ride to get us to the hotel. It isn't that far

from here; we can settle in and get some dinner at the hotel instead of finding somewhere on the way."

"Yeh, that sounds fine." I agree with Femi as all I am anxious to do is have a bit of privacy in the bathroom with a toilet and have no one standing outside the door scrutinising every sound coming from it. "How long will it take?"

"About 20 minutes or so. But the traffic, hopefully, will be light so should be quicker," Femi answers and I notice how, as per usual, the heat does not affect him whatsoever. He is as calm as ever and, in fact, seems more at ease in this environment than back in London.

Femi sits in the front passenger seat while I bundle in the back. The fake leather seats stick to my trousers and t-shirt as I sit back. I roll down both windows but all that rushes in is hot, humid air. The streets are so busy everywhere. People are still out rushing around and all the shops are open with lights and sounds coming from all directions. The traffic on the street is busier than London it seems, and this is supposed to be a quiet time according to the driver and Femi.

"So, what is the plan tomorrow?" As soon as I asked the question, I was reminded that I am sure Femi would not want to discuss the aspects of our itinerary in the presence of a stranger.

Femi looks over his shoulder, towards my direction in the back of the car.

"We can go through everything once we get to the hotel. How are you adjusting to the heat of Luxor?"

His response obviously also reminds me of the covert aspects of some discussions between us.

"Ah, where are you from?" The driver's voice comes

in my direction. He speaks with a strong accent but his English is excellent.

"From London, England." I have no idea why I felt I had to explain London was in England, but just in case another London was well known somewhere.

The driver lets out a laugh at my answer.

"Ah, the city of grey clouds and rain."

"You have been there then, I take it, from your comment?"

"Oh no," the driver answers as he stops at a red light. The beads on his rear-view mirror swing and I can just make out a photograph of two children hanging from them. "I am not lucky enough to go to London as yet, but hopefully my children will get to study there at some point."

Yet another person who thinks London is a lucky place, full of opportunities and forever making people's dreams come true. How disillusioned the world can be at times.

"So, your friend tells me you are here to see as much of the sights as possible along the Nile, starting in Luxor."

So, Femi has come up with a story already with the driver. I suppose that was the conversation he was having at the car as I waited for him.

I play along with the narrative.

"Yes, that is correct. It is my first time here and I have always wanted to see the culture and history of this beautiful country."

As the car moves off from the red light, the driver pulls out a cigarette packet from his front shirt pocket, pulls one out with his mouth and offers one to Femi and I. We both decline.

"Just be careful of all the crooks that this beautiful

country has to offer. They will see you coming from a distance." A gentle warning from him to me.

We pull up outside this small hotel, which looks more like a bed and breakfast type of place. A neon green sign over the doorway says 'Rooms'. I must admit, I am slightly disappointed as I was hoping for a five-star hotel, but I knew that was being too hopeful since all the expenses are paid for me on this trip, so it is logical things would have an economical feel to them.

Femi settles the fee with the driver and we bid him thanks and goodbye. I hope Femi was not expecting me to pay as I have not discussed these points with him about how we keep track of who pays for what, but I assume he will take the lead on all this. I must remember to bring it up and offer at some point, just so he does not think I am taking liberties.

Thankfully, we have separate rooms, another aspect that concerned me when we booked in, as I do not think I could fully relax sharing a room with Femi. The room is small, cramped and very sparse with the most minimal aspects of what is needed for a stay. I overheard Femi checking us in for one night only so I assume we are travelling elsewhere tomorrow, but I will ask all the details at dinner that we will have downstairs in about 30 minutes or so.

There is no point in unpacking all of my clothes, then again, there is only one bag and it contains the bare minimum for our trip, as was explained by Femi when we left London. The bathroom could be easily mistaken for a wardrobe due to the minimal space around the toilet, shower cubicle with cloth curtain around it and hand basin in the corner. It's fine, it's for one night and I am not paying for it. There is no air conditioning, however, and it's useless having the window open as I am not sure what is warmer, inside or outside the room.

"How is your room?" Femi is already downstairs in the dining area where there are four circular tables spaced out. We are the only two present in the room.

"It's good. Need to ask the reception desk if there is a fan I can borrow overnight, as I do not think I will be able to sleep at all with the heat."

I pull out a seat opposite Femi. He dwarfs the table and the chair, as always.

"I have a feeling this is not going to be the last time I hear you complain of the heat out here." Femi pours me a glass of water from the closed bottle of water on the table. "I have already taken the liberty of ordering us some dinner. I hope that's OK. I have stayed away from anything too exciting or exotic that will play up your stomach."

Damn, how did Femi sense I have bowel issues? Well, at least it is out in the open now.

Femi's body slants towards the table. His face is now more serious than before. The scar on the side of his face gives him a commanding look, slightly intimidating if you did not know the gentler side to this man.

"I have been in contact with someone about where we have to go tomorrow. For the inspection of 'it'."

I understand we will be talking in code while we sit here.

"That's good. So, is it tomorrow that I get to see the paint–" Before I can finish the word, I promptly change the ending of my sentence to '…it? Get to see it?"

Femi rolls his eyes slightly.

"It seems we will go to the house tomorrow. It is not that

far from here, but I may get a hire car so at least we don't have to rely on transport, just in case plans and timings change."

Femi looks over to the direction of the doorway and it seems he is satisfied that no one is coming and, indeed, that no one can hear us.

"Tell me – not in great detail – but how will you know 'it' is what 'it' is supposed to be?"

This is the first time that Femi has wanted to ask about what I will do to authenticate that the painting is the original one that was presumed destroyed. Surely his boss already has confidence in what I can do otherwise I would not be on this trip in the first place. I presume they are now aware of the photograph and timeline and how that aspect of the research and evidence I pulled together over time can be put forward as an argument that the painting is still in circulation. The only hint of how I would validate it as being the real painting is how the dating of the characteristic blue paints were mixed back then.

"It's all to do with the colour blue on this particular artefact."

Femi motions with his head and raises an eyebrow in a look of confusion.

"The colour was challenging for Vincent to mix up back then due to his vision problems. So, in my research, I spent extensive time looking at how he would, over time, have had various failed attempts to get the blue colour to a stage of brilliance that would stand out for him to see while he painted, but also so that it captured the essence of the emotion of the flower."

"I still don't follow."

Despite the shower, I was already so warm and sweating

again. I wore a half-sleeve checked shirt and had to undo my top three buttons, but it was still useless. As I undid the buttons, it took me back to the days when she would undo my top shirt buttons as she preferred my look that way. I shake that memory from my mind.

"Well, I will be able to use the blue colour on the pa… 'it' to provide an age for it. That will obviously give you the date it was created."

"Fascinating." Femi sat back in his chair with an air of achievement about him.

"I have everything with me that is required to carry out the procedure and I have tested it time and time again, in London, with various works. The dating accuracy rate is pretty much 100% in all attempts."

Femi nods in understanding.

"The only thing is, I hope the owners, the family who have it, understand that I will need to scrape one corner of it to obtain a sample."

Femi smiles and folds his arms across his chest. He spreads his legs out in front of him from the side of the table.

"Oh, I am sure they will be absolutely fine with it."

I look over my shoulder and notice our dinner being brought over to the table, with the conversation coming to an end, just in time.

26

Before

The sleep was not too bad considering it was like a million degrees in the bedroom. I did not manage to get a fan for the room and, in fact, when I asked the reception staff for one last night they looked at me like I had just asked for a spaceship to travel to space. I dreamt of being physically in the presence of the painting. To actually be up close with the masterpiece. I have to keep the doubts away from my mind that the painting may not be the real thing. But I am so confident that if it *is* the real thing, I will prove it by the dating of the paint.

I am to meet Femi downstairs for breakfast at 8.00 AM and have managed to set an alarm of some sort on my watch but, in the end, it was not needed as the sun was up bright and early through the blinds and had dragged me out of bed.

"How was the sleep for the London man?"

"I am not sure what use having a shower was." I pull the chair out of direct sunlight and sit on the opposite side of the table from Femi. "I am sweating already and I have only just come downstairs," I hear myself speak and I wonder if Femi is getting sick and tired of me complaining of the heat, but then again, what did he expect from me?

We choose a light breakfast consisting of strong black coffee and some pastries that bloat me as soon as I take a couple of mouthfuls. I ask myself, *"How can they affect me so quickly and the only thing that I can put my finger on is that it is probably a psychosomatic symptom that I have?"*

"So, what is the plan today? What time do we get to see it, then?" I am continuing to be aware of the fact that we refer to the painting in some form of code word when out in the open. Gives me the sensation of being in a spy movie.

"I will be in contact with the family later this morning to arrange all the details."

That one sentence from Femi reminds me that he told me not to bring a mobile phone on the trip. The reasoning was due to some aspect of security, but I did not fully understand his reasoning but went along with it anyway. At first, it was a strange sensation not having a phone with me and not being connected to things all the time but, eventually, it actually became quite liberating. My concern was that I would need to reach out to Fiona if I ended up having some form of crisis or stupid thought process that started to consume me, but, so far, it's all been OK.

"Have you got everything that you need for the examination?"

Femi makes it sound like I am doing a post-mortem on a specimen.

"Yes, I have all I need. The main aspect I need is to be alone with it, *in peace.*" I emphasise the last few words as I want to savour the time with the painting.

"Oh, don't worry, Hugo, you will have all the time you need with it." I look directly at Femi and he notices me raise my eyebrow. "Alone with it. Undisturbed."

"Hugo, I will be back in a few minutes. I just want to go and check on how close the destination is. Wait here for me and then we can go through the plan for the day."

I resist having any more bread that is laid out in front of me. I also know that the strong black coffee will make me use the toilet again and I would need to fully empty my bowels before we set off. I really do hope it kicks in as the flight made me feel very sluggish and the last thing I want to do is have to use a toilet while out and about or, even worse, while we are with the painting. That would be extremely embarrassing and would knock my concentration all over the place.

"You no like the breakfast?" The lovely lady who laid the table for us walks in carrying even more pastries and treats. She walks with a slight shuffling gait with small steps. I would guess she is probably in her 60s and has spent all her life working to make others at ease. Be that her own family or people like me who do not have the stomach to enjoy the amazing treats she brings.

"No, no, the food is very lovely. It is just too much for this time of day for me. I have never been used to having much food in the morning and often skip breakfast." My attempt to make her feel at ease I think helped as I did not want to offend her or her efforts at making me feel welcome.

She starts clearing the table away and I feel compelled to help. But she ushers me away with her hands.

I was half waiting for her to say something back to me, but she just shuffled back out of the room carrying a tray full of pastries and bread that is mostly untouched.

Femi is still not back and I remember I have a folded up print of the painting in my pocket. I wanted to show

Femi what the world feels the painting may look like. I lay the print on the table, ensuring no one is coming back into the room. The striking beauty of this depiction is the deep rich blue used. The colour and gradual build up of the layers to bring the painting into its emotional being is just so beautiful to imagine. Although this is just a print, even this shows how the painting wants to talk to us. How even on a flat surface, the light catches the small delicate brush strokes to make the colours ripple the surface and want to come into your world. It shows the dramatic contrast of the yellow sunflower heads wanting to escape the navy background and grow and reach the sky. It gives the impression of the flowers being reborn in that moment. The flowers want to break away from the shackled entrapment to a greater sense of fulfilment, reflecting the density that they feel they have the right to have ownership over. I can only imagine what Vincent's mind and inner torment was fighting when he painted this.

I feel the characteristically slightly uncomfortable abdominal bloating and cramping setting in from the strong black coffee. This is a welcome feeling as I can use the toilet in my room with no interruption and take my sweet time. There is no sign of Femi as yet; I am sure he will know that I have gone back to the room if he returns.

A good 11 minutes of relaxing peace allows me to be set up for the day now. I remember seeing a gastroenterologist a few years ago because I was paranoid that I might have had bowel cancer due to my lack of gastric transit. But after all the investigations, mainly having a shiny flexible camera being put up my butt and, who knows, streamed all over the Internet on some TikTok or Snapchat platform, but the amazing diagnosis was that I have irritable bowel syndrome. So, basically, I have a temperamental gut that reflects my temperamental mind. I am sure the two are connected. I recall some literature I read somewhere suggesting the link between unsettled traumas in life and how they can present in adulthood as physical illness and symptoms in the body. According to this paper, the main physical symptoms were headaches, chest pain with palpitations, dizziness, abdominal cramps and change in bowel habit, mainly constipation. After reading this, it should have given me some insight and settled me a bit, but this was not the case. At least it's not the big, fucking C-word of diagnosis.

I really want to change into another t-shirt as this one's already sweat-soaked, but I suppose I will no doubt need to change again later in the day, so I will hold off for now. There is no knock on the door so far, which means Femi either is not back or he is being a mind reader and polite again and knows I am doing my business in the 'office'.

"Hey, you should have come and knocked on my room when you got back. Have you been back long?" I see Femi sitting back at the table as I get downstairs. He has his phone out, scrolling through something and there is a key on the table.

"I just got back. So, I got us a hire car; it will be easier if we have our own transport."

"Any update on when we get to visit it?" I am anxious to do what we are here to do now.

"Yes, sure. So, the family have been in contact." There was another pause from Femi like he was trying to work out the next sentence and what more to tell me. He looked back down at the screen on his phone like the answer to the rest of his sentence would suddenly jump out at him.

I feel I have to prompt him.

"And...?"

"They will be moving it to another location after we view it, but the only window we have is this evening." Femi quickly puts his phone away in his pocket and he notices me glance over at the screen.

He continues, this time with a more relaxed look to him and a smile on his face. Everything now seems back to the calm, controlled Femi.

"...Which means we have time in the day to relax and take in a bit of Luxor. The only thing we need to do now is check out, so make sure you bring your bag down with you."

"We not staying here this evening then?" Of course we are not. As soon as I asked, I heard how stupid I must have sounded.

"No, we will be staying elsewhere tonight, depending on how you get on with the examination later."

There isn't much more I can say to that. I can tell from Femi's tone that he does not want to say much more about it.

"Sounds good. Aren't the Luxor Temple and the Valley of the Kings nearby?"

Femi shows off that dazzling smile he has. The scar on the side of his face has become an inviting and endearing feature rather than one that represents perhaps pain in the past.

"I take it you want a tourist's day out to fill the time, right?"

"Of course, man. Why come to Egypt and not get to see all the greatness it has to offer?"

Femi stretches his long limbs and yawns.

"Well, if you can stand the heat, then let's go show you Egypt."

The damn heat.

27

Before

The car's windows are open, all four of them, but still everything sticks to the seats with the heat. I can feel my chinos and boxers so uncomfortably as I sit in the passenger seat next to Femi. He drove us here, in the hire car, this evening. I have the opportunity to test my amazing replica military watch light up in the dark. I find the side button and a green glow lights up the face of the watch. The time is 11.17 PM I am still baffled as to why we are having this meeting so late in the night, but Femi insisted that the family only had this window of time before they travelled again with the painting.

We are parked on the street. It seems this is a private road leading to the private estates that line either side of the road with their gated driveways.

"Which house is it?" I scan the impressive mansion fronted houses amongst the immaculate green lush gardens lit with lights, even at this hour. Sprinklers are twisting away giving much-needed hydration to the plants. I can't help but fantasise diving headfirst into the jet of water to cool me down.

There is no answer from Femi. I look over to him and see how he is tapping his fingers on the steering wheel with his gaze out of the window to the gates across the street.

"Femi? All OK?"

"Yes, yes. Sorry, I was miles away. What were you saying?"

"Which house are we going to? It's like a sauna in here and I'm keen to get into the air conditioning of the house."

Femi raises his hand and points to the house over to the far end of the street.

"That one over there with the stone lion statues outside the gates."

I lean over to get a better look at the direction of Femi's finger.

"The one with all the lights off. You sure they are in and expecting us?"

Perhaps the property spirals out behind the main front that we can't see and everyone is in the back. That's probably why the front is in darkness.

"Why have you parked all the way over here then? Get us closer."

"Hugo!"

I am taken aback by Femi's bark towards me.

"Sorry. I didn't mean to shout. I just need to think for a minute, please."

"Yeh. Sure. Whatever, man."

I get out of the car and walk round to the back. It's no cooler outside, but I can let my chinos air for a bit. There is a deafening silence to the street. The only intermittent sound is that of the odd mosquito buzzing by and a low hum of the street lamp that is a good few feet away. Whatever is going on with Femi, I think I should let him deal with it, alone.

This would be the perfect time to get a cigarette out

from my trouser pocket, light one and lean on the car and smoke it. I would pull slow meaningful drags from it and blow the smoke out slowly while easing my mind and the heated situation. The only thing wrong with that though is that I have never smoked. But it feels like the right situation in which to. Or perhaps that's me attaching too much to what I see on Netflix.

Femi swings open the driver's door and unwinds his torso from the car.

"Hugo. Let me go check on the house first. You wait here."

"Check on the house? What do you mean? The house is right there!" My voice is slightly irritated and I think Femi can sense that.

"I mean, let me go and see if we have indeed got the right time and day for this. I mean, it seems there is no one in." Femi leans on the car and keeps his gaze firmly fixed on the house.

If I did not know I was in Luxor, this street could easily be placed in California or Dubai with how it is laid out. The presence and grandeur of the design of the street just exhales wealth. I feel that I do not have the energy to disagree with Femi at this stage. I have to trust whatever he says and his thought process on this. I am just here to have my time to examine the artefact and to give my interpretation with any research that I have done over the years. My paperwork is in the car, so I will wait for Femi to give me the all clear to come to the house with it all when he is ready.

"Sure, I mean, it is late at night so I was surprised that we were meeting them at this time. You do realise that it will take me some time to fully carry out my inspection of the piece." I reminded Femi that I would need a few hours alone with the painting. Part of that is for selfish reasons. I can't come that close to the masterpiece and not have my time alone with it. To feel the emotion and capture the essence of such a master at work. To know that his hands, his fingers, his eyes, his words surrounded and engulfed the painting all those years ago.

"Femi." He is fixated on the house again and does not answer. He seems startled and looks over at my voice, like he has just noticed me for the first time, standing here with him. His face is in darkness. With his stature and with not clearly seeing his facial expression, he appears menacing.

"Yes, Hugo, sorry; of course. The time you need with the painting. You will need uninterrupted time with it and with your research."

"Good; just so that you know, it's..." I flip my wrist over and press the side button to illuminate the face of it again, "...it's nearly morning."

"Perhaps I can convince them to let us come at a decent time during the day. Yes, that seems like the better plan. I will go and put that to them. Good thinking, Hugo."

Femi has a more hurried nature to his voice now, which is so out of character.

"Wait here, Hugo, and I will be back as quick as I can."

I give an unimpressed look back at him. He moves a step closer to me. Now I can see his facial expression better. It is gentle. I feel the weight of his hand on my shoulder as he continues to reassure me and maintain the trust built up in him and the safety that he has created for me.

"Everything is OK, Hugo. Please trust me. I will go and explain that we need more time during the day with it and I am sure they will understand. You take the weight off your feet and rest here for a bit." He flashes one of his smiles at me, allowing his white immaculate teeth to shine through the darkness.

I prop myself against the car, watching Femi walk over to the house. The further he gets, the smaller his presence becomes and he now seems more of an average person, someone who would not show me up in public with his build. I always feel so insignificant when I stand next to him.

I try to concentrate on where he is going. The road curves slightly and the house's entrance gates are obscured by the stone lion statues and the tall bush trees on either side. Femi disappears from view as he passes the first stone lion.

I may as well make use of the time and check all my papers in the car's boot. I pop it open and see the papers scattered all over the place. Damn, the ride here is at fault of causing that. I should have ensured they were held down better. I take another peek over the lid of the boot in the direction of the house to see if there is any sign of Femi. Nothing at all yet.

My attention back to the papers in the boot, I gather them up and try to maintain the order I had put them in earlier. I see the black, rolled up casing tucked in the corner of the boot. It resembles camping equipment, like a sleeping bag or tent. This, Femi told me, was required in case we need to transport the painting anywhere for further examination. I was always under the impression that the painting was not to be moved due to the security ramifications, which Femi assured me that was not really needed, as we would not be moving the painting. But it was good to be well prepared. There were so many aspects to consider when transporting paintings like this – the climate, the heat exposure, the UV radiation, the humidity, the salt content and on and on. But, as Femi explained, we would not need to transport the painting. It was just in case. But the protective casing seems very technical and from what I have read about it, it will stand up to the job of protecting the painting if, indeed, we *do* ever need to transport it. It comes with all the bells and whistles.

I gather up all my papers as best as I can and make a nice, secure pile in the corner of the boot. I wedge my bags on either side to keep them from falling all over the place again. Closing the boot, I keep my eyes over to the direction of where Femi disappeared. Still no sign of movement. I return to sit in the passenger seat of the car.

It seems cooler in the car now. Perhaps because I have become acclimatised to the heat outside the car. I feel my chinos are better fitting now and not stuck and riding up my buttocks. The car seat feels a lot more comfortable now. Comfortable in the manner that I can rest my eyes for a while. Just a bit, while Femi does what he needs to do. Looking around, outside the car, up and down the road, there is stillness. It seems to be a very safe, secure neighbourhood. A little nap will be absolutely safe and fine to have here. I will use my fake fancy watch to set an alarm. Who am I kidding? There is no way to work out how to set an alarm on this thing. I never read any instruction manuals that come with devices. I mean, who ever does?

The heat around me seems very comforting now and is making my eyelids heavy. Let's see how far back I can put the chair in here. There is always a little excitement when thinking about having a nap on travels. Those first few minutes of settling in the seat and exploring the various possible positions to get comfortable. I decide to face straight up on my back with my arms folded across my chest, for now. The type a corpse would have in a casket. Great thought.

I wake with a start. Was that a gunshot I heard, a firework or a car exhaust backfiring? I jolt upright. Looking around, everything seems so still. I remember where I am, sitting in the car, on this street, in Luxor. My face feels damp and I remove the sweat from my forehead with my hand. Now I remember – Femi. Femi went to the house to ask if we can return tomorrow to inspect the painting. Glancing at my watch, I am sure he has been gone for over an hour. I hope all is OK.

My neck is stiff from the rest and the position I was lying in. I feel the pressure on my bladder, as I need to take a piss. Had I known he would be as long as this, I would have gone before we had left. I get out the car and go to a bush at the side of the road.

What, is that Femi running towards me? What the hell! What is he carrying?

"Hugo. Get in the car. Now!"

The closer Femi gets, the more urgency I witness in his actions. In the middle of the road, I start to move towards him, but he shouts more instructions.

"Open the back door, quickly!"

I get in, slide across to the other side and pull the handle to release the car door and Femi gets close enough for me to see a rectangular object carried in his arms. It has what appears to be a thick cloth covering it.

"Go over to the other side and pull it over, gently."

I do as I am told. Femi closes the door after pushing the

object slowly onto the back seat. I motion to get out.

"Hurry Hugo! We need to get going! Make sure it is secure in the back!"

I feel the car suspension fall under the stress of Femi's weight as he gets into the driver seat. He starts the car, makes a smooth U-turn in the road and we go back the way we came.

28

Before

Femi drove with purpose. He was out of breath when he got in the car and there was sweat pouring from his forehead. I had not seen him like this before. His driving had an urgency, although driving in Luxor is always with purpose and a fair amount of stress. Well, it all seems stressful to an outsider like me, but this is on another level with Femi. The roads were quiet in the fancy neighbourhood, but as we got nearer to the city centre it became hazardous in the traffic, both with vehicles and pedestrians.

I daren't speak while we drove. For no other reason but I wanted to stay alive in the car with his driving. It was a hire car that Femi had sourced earlier in the day. I was not with him when he went to pick it up. I was instructed to rest and to keep all our belongings close to me. We had checked out of the small motel that we spent one night in and Femi had explained that we would be staying elsewhere tonight. Now I see why we could not stay at the same motel. This all seems very wrong.

As we speed through the night of Luxor, the glow of the street-lamps pass in quick succession by the car window. There are draughts of sand dune dust around the halo of the lamps. The air is still warm, but with the speed of

Femi's driving and the twists and turns we are taking, it's allowing some degree of breeze to float into the car and ease the temperature. The sounds become so much more prominent at night. The car horns never seem to end, be it day or night. I now become more aware of how many people hang around on the streets at night. Perhaps it is due to the intense heat during the day that many wait until sundown to venture out. The street still has many shop fronts open and the bazaars are vibrant with the commotion of people.

I have no idea where we were headed now, but I need to be confident that Femi has this all in hand and is part of the arrangements. Then I remember what was placed on the back seat of the car and the fearful expression on Femi's face as he raced to the car holding it. It could only be one thing that he carried out of that house. Only one thing that has that shape and size. My mind reaches all sorts of conclusions, each one as ludicrous as the next. But then again, this isn't exactly a normal situation to be in, so the ludicrous aspect of it seems very much in keeping with the situation.

We come to a stop at a red traffic light. Finally, there seem to be some moments to allow us to stop and breathe and take it all in.

Femi sits with both hands on the steering wheel, looking straight ahead.

"So. You want to tell me what this is all about?" I use this time to get him to explain.

I watch him, sitting there, waiting for the lights to change.

His breathing is getting steadier now. The sweat has disappeared from his forehead, as it is not glistening from the glare of the lights anymore.

"What was that you said?" Femi's voice seems different to any tone I have heard in the past. He sounds detached. Sounds as though he is not actually here.

The lights change to green and he moves off slowly. Much calmer now. I do not repeat my question, as I am sure he heard perfectly well what I had asked. I look out the window and watch the night life of Luxor go past again.

"There is a change in arrangements. Last-minute thing. You know how it is sometimes." Femi does not show any emotion in his voice. It is flat and monotonous in nature.

"No, Femi, I do not know how it is sometimes. Why don't you educate me on that?" I remain looking out the window with my response. I am grateful for the breeze growing stronger through the car.

We come to a crossroads; Femi looks both ways, lingers with his gaze and works out which way to turn. Now I have to ask the question myself, how does Femi actually know where he is going, here in Luxor? Unless he has been here before or studied his route prior to tonight.

"Where are we going, Femi?" He decides to take a right. "For fuck's sake, Femi. Talk to me. What the hell is going on?"

I sit here staring at him while he keeps driving with his eyes fixed firmly on the road. I see the reflection of the streetlights flashing over his face as we pass them by. I feel like punching him right now, right there on the side of his face until he speaks to me. We suddenly turn off the main road into a dark alleyway. The sharp turn catches me unaware and my left elbow crashes into the side of the door handle. Femi pulls the car to a stop on the side of the road away from any lights and turns the engine off.

He sits there with his hands still on the steering wheel and lets out a big sigh. I watch him as he lets his head kick back and rest on the headrest.

"Hugo. There has been a slight development. Well, unforeseen development."

"No shit, Sherlock!" my automatic reply thunders out of my mouth. As soon as I speak the words I know that perhaps Femi wouldn't understand that saying. "Tell me; what is all this?" We sit there in darkness. Femi looks straight ahead out of the front windscreen while I face him sitting in the passenger seat. To my right, just through the gap between the two front seats of the car, I can see, lying on the back seat, the rectangular painting or, of course, what I assume to be *the* painting.

Femi still avoids eye contact. He nods with his head to the object behind us.

"I am sure you know what that is. It's the *Sunflowers*."

"What the fuck, Femi! Why have you got it? Why is it in the car?" My voice is agitated now and even more so with the lack of moving ventilation in the car since we have come to a standstill.

"It wasn't safe there anymore. You see…" He stalls and then shifts in his seat to face me. "You see, the reason why we had to come now, urgently, is because the family were worried that others knew of its existence. Others who have been trying to get hold of the painting ever since it left Japan, before the bombing."

"Who, Femi? Who has been trying to get hold of the painting?"

Femi places his hands on either side of his face, showing his frustration at the situation also.

"Well, I am sure you know where most of the art from

that period was headed to and *by* whom."

"Which period do you mean? The war – as in at the time of World War Two, is that what you mean?" He nods in agreement. "You mean to say that the Nazis are hunting this painting, now, in this day and age? What the hell, man." I can feel the heat rising from my chest to my neck and the sweat just encasing every inch of my skin. I go to open the door to get some air but he cries out.

"No, Hugo! We need to keep moving now. It isn't safe here at the moment. We need to get out of this car and get the painting safely back into the casing that we have in the back."

"Wait. You knew all this time, Femi; is that why you brought the casing with you? You knew about this all along."

"No, Hugo. I did *not* know it was like this until I got into the house and spoke to the family. They literally forced me to take the painting. They knew I had you with me and that we have contacts to get the painting safe."

"What do you mean 'contacts'? It's just you and me." I keep needing to wipe the salty sweat from my eyes as it drips from my forehead, while Femi still looks calm and in control over there.

"I called my boss; they have been briefed of the situation and it's agreed that we will transport the painting to a curator in Cairo and it will be safe there."

This is getting worse and worse. Now it seems we really are going onto an Indiana Jones type crusade across Egypt. Fucking hell! What is this? I say it out loud.

"Fucking hell! What is this?"

"Look, Hugo. This isn't what I signed up for either. But we are here now. I told you to trust me. Nothing will come to harm you. But, we need to be a team now. This is up to us."

"How about—" Femi cuts me off.

"The authorities. Is that what you were about to ask? Well, we don't know how far the hunters have infiltrated. They could have every aspect of the police here looking for us already."

This is the first time it hits me that perhaps we have also become prey among this chase.

"What do you mean by 'us', Femi? How do they know we are here and who we are?"

Femi moves as if to start the car up.

"Femi, do they know who I am?"

He pauses.

"No. But it's only a matter of time until they know the painting is not there anymore. And when they do, they will be tracking it, with all their resources. Which is why we need to get this car as far away from *us* as possible and get to Cairo safely." He starts the car up.

The drive is now smoother than before we stopped. We both sit in silence, digesting everything that has just been said.

"They won't be able to track the hire car. I used fake documents to hire it out, so we can just dump it on the way."

"Of course you did, Femi. Nothing surprises me anymore. What else did you do? Use infrared sniper guns to get the painting?" Femi is not impressed by my comments and indicates this by kissing his teeth at me.

We sit in silence again for a while. The time is getting on to the early hours and it will be dawn soon.

"So, what exactly is the plan?"

"We both need rest. It will help me think. We will dump the car, get all our belongings and secure it in the casing." By 'it', I am sure Femi means the painting. It is like if he does not mention it by name it will not attract direct attention.

"I will find a safe way to get us to Cairo, Hugo. Please don't worry."

Yeh, right; not to worry. You are asking someone who has had years of therapy not to worry. Good luck with that one.

29

Before

We sat in silence; me in the passenger seat looking at the changing landscape of Luxor passing by and Femi driving, which, at times, seemed like he was going round in circles, but I assume he was ensuring no one was following us. Dawn was approaching fast and the colours of the sky reflected this and the soothing sounds at this time made their presence heard. There was a dog barking, various farm animals giving their morning calls and the odd tractor firing up, ready for some honest work. As the buildings got sparser in nature, more of the distant horizon was coming into view.

No more busy shop fronts with the hustle of people. All the shutters were still drawn. No more colourful bazaars selling everything from fabrics to vegetables. Those places were now empty and lonely in their own presence. It had been close to 45 minutes of driving without us saying a word. I am determined not to give in first. I had way too much of that back then. With her, it was always me who would reach out first and apologise. To be fair, in most of the occasions, it *was* my fault for the negativity caused. But here, with Femi, he needs to step up and take responsibility.

"I had no choice and time was against us, Hugo."

As if by telepathy, Femi responds to my thoughts.

"What do you mean, against 'us'? I had no knowledge of or part in what you did back there." Hearing myself, the 45 minutes of silence has not calmed me at all.

"You should have seen the look on the family's faces there. They were just so frightened when they were telling me about the suspicions of people coming to claim the painting."

I need him to tell me exactly what he knows now that he has decided to speak.

"Tell me exactly what you were told in there. You owe me that much."

He stops the car at the end of a crossroads and looks in both directions. I catch a look at his expression as he looks past me, along the road. He looks less anxious than when he got into the car, but there is still a lack of the calm and controlled look on his face as was in London.

"We will need to leave the car somewhere and then make our way on foot. We can find an abandoned building to get a few hours' rest while I make the arrangements to get us to Cairo."

He takes the right and drives slowly along the road. There are only a few single-storey buildings on this road, interspersed with land that seems to have a mixture of waste land and cultivated farm land. A few dogs are wandering around and they stop to take notice of us driving, watching us closely with their inquisitive eyes.

Femi pulls up to the side of the road and parks a few feet behind a row of cars.

"We can leave the car here. It does not look too suspicious being here for a few hours," he says while switching off the engine. "Let's get the painting into the casing, get our bags and make way on foot. We can get a bit of distance between the car and us before getting some rest."

He opens the door, gets out to walk around to the car's boot and pops it open. I can feel him rummaging around in the back. In the wing mirror's reflection on the driver's side, I see that he pulls out the casing rolled up in the corner of the boot. I also notice him bend over onto the dusty floor to lay the casing out flat. I remain seated like a spoiled child having a tantrum.

"Hugo, please. We can't be out here in the open much longer. I need your help. It needs both of us. Please, " Femi pleads as he leans in from the open window. His torso fills the whole frame. I picture him getting stuck in it with the dogs outside barking and biting at his ankles.

"Hugo!" I snap back to the here and now at the sound of my name. "Look, I will explain once we get somewhere not so exposed. Now, please come and help me."

In an act of frustration, I fling open my door, get out the car and walk around to Femi, dragging my feet and kicking up dust everywhere. Fuck it; I will be a child if that's how he wants to play this at this time.

I see the black casing on the floor, with all manner of brackets and fasteners and locks and zips spread out. As I walk closer, I can make out several layers and compartments to this casing. The material seems to have various aspects to it also.

"What the hell is that?"

"It is a state-of-the-art protective material to keep artefacts at the optimum hydration, temperature and exposure to light, to allow transit of the artefact."

"You memorised that well from the information manual, I see." I am being as flippant as I can.

I notice how the dawn light is rapidly making everything around us seem so much brighter. Whatever the real reason for us to have this painting, I think I need to help Femi get it into this casing so we can both get out of sight. I have to trust what he is saying.

It takes us a good 20 minutes or so to go through the checks of the casing on the floor. Femi has obviously been trained in this. There was a certain order that things had to be done. This was even before we could get the painting into it.

"Once we get it into the casing, we should not need to open the casing again until we get to meet the curator. But we will need to check every aspect of the outer perimeter of the enclosure along our journey." There again, Femi mentions this curator. I will not push with all my questions. As much as I want to kick Femi in the head right now, I need him to get us somewhere safe and quick.

"You ready?" Femi nods over to me at the rear of the car and to the painting and opens the back door. "I will pull it out first and then you take the other end of the weight as I pull it. OK?" I nod and walk over to stand behind Femi at the open door. As Femi pulls it out, I see that a thick red cloth surrounds it. There is no area of the painting showing at all. As I get hold of the end with Femi pulling, I feel that I am potentially holding something that was considered destroyed. A legend in itself. I concentrate on the weight of it in my hands, wanting to ensure I do not drop it but at the same time not wishing to apply too much pressure as to cause any harm to it – almost like it is a living being.

"You got it – got the weight? Now move round and rotate it so it faces up and lower it with me into the middle of the casing."

I do not speak while I concentrate on the pace, movement and directions from Femi. Gravel shifts below my shoes as I shuffle around the casing on the floor. I lower the painting down to keep it steady and even, while Femi does the same. In the corner of my eye, I spot a couple of the stray dogs standing, ever so still, analysing our movements. No time to let my concentration wander around me. Finally, it is resting flat in the middle of the black casing on the floor. I can tell Femi made the ground flat, devoid of any stones, before laying the casing open.

"Perfect. Well done, Hugo."

Why did that sound so patronising from him? In any other circumstance, it would have been a welcome comment from Femi, but the way I am feeling at present makes me sound a little pathetic.

The morning's heat has started already and I feel the sweat beads forming again on my face and neck.

"Right, let's close this up and get it attached to our backs."

"Attached to *our* backs; what do you mean?"

"We will take turns carrying it. See these buckles...." Femi crouches down and picks up one of the harnesses, "... these will secure it on our back so we can keep it safe. We will take turns in carrying it."

Great. I was nervous enough just pulling it out of the car. How the hell does he expect me to stay calm and in control with it on my back?

I stand back while studying Femi closing the casing with all its zips, buckles, locks and compartments. There seems to be a certain order he is following and I will leave him to it, unless he instructs me to do something. I am conscious of how the light is now and that soon people will be walking around this road, I am sure.

"Hugo, come down here with me. We need to go through the edges to make sure it is all secure." Femi pads the floor next to him indicating me to crouch down there. "So, all the edges need to be airtight so that every time we carry the case and stop for a break, we need to inspect it at regular intervals to ensure all the seams are intact." He runs his thick, smooth fingers along the top edge, following the tight zip mesh line. He continues, "Because any leak in the seal could potentially cause damage to it inside."

No idea why he keeps referring to the painting as 'it'. We don't need to now. We take our time checking all four sides of the casing. Femi leads and I follow, checking the same side afterwards to agree it all looks tight and in place.

We both sit there for a minute, on the floor, surrounded by stones, dust and sand with a masterpiece at our feet.

"What the fuck, Femi! What *is* all this? Only a few days ago we were out hitting the city of London, laughing, at ease. Now look at us." My shoulders slump and I place my head in my hands.

"This isn't great. I get that, Hugo. But it will not be long now. Just need to find a plan and stick with it. You will be back in London in no time."

Somehow, Femi's words were not all that reassuring to me at this moment.

"Come on, let's get going; get the bags out from the back and I will do the first carry. I will direct you on how to handle it and get it onto my back and get all the buckles and harnesses in place."

As he gets up, he places a hand on my shoulder to remind me that he is still my friend perhaps, or that he is calling all the shots here now. I do not know anymore. This is not good for me at all.

"Femi?"

"Yes, Hugo, what is it?"

"What if I want to go back to London now? What if I just give the money back paid to me for any work outstanding? You have the painting now and you seem to know the plan to get to this curator in Cairo. Surely this can now be done without me?"

"Hugo, I'm afraid we really don't have a say in this now. Come on, let's get on with it."

30

Before

"How was your first trip to Egypt, Hugo?"

"Oh, it was great. Amazing. I wish I had had more time there. I mean, we got to see the sights, experience all the great aspects of Luxor, like the hot humidity inside of a taxi, the amazing night in a step down from a bed and breakfast, oh, and not to forget the amazing experience of literally being dragged around Luxor in the middle of the night, not knowing what the fuck I was doing and then being forced to conceal a painting that is probably worth more than anything I have and will ever come close to having. So, yes, it was amazing, thank you."

I can just imagine the conversation that will take place when I get back home to London. I mean, who will I have this conversation with? Probably just Fiona in our next therapy session. The amount of triggers I will be able to discuss with her that have occurred on this trip and I have a horrible feeling that there are more to come. I have that unsettled, shaky feeling that sits deep within me; it lets itself know, bit by bit, but not too much so that it allows the outside world to relate to it. Oh no, the fucking monster wants to cause just enough chaos inside me to make me feel fucked around everyone else.

I keep a few paces behind Femi, as he carries the

package, our loot, on his back. The sun is in full force now and the streets are getting busy. Femi leads us as much off the main pedestrian areas as possible, cutting through alleys and then open barren land that spreads for ages with its sand dunes, mixed with the odd outhouse at times.

The locals let us be. They give the odd glance here and there, but mainly they keep focused on what they are doing or where they are going. Many seem like farmers and are going to the fields for the morning crop rotation perhaps. Others are carrying, pushing or pulling boxes, crates, trolleys and all manner in-between. I suspect they are en route to set up all the bazaars that we keep passing. But what do I know, pretending to know every aspect of this land just to make me feel a little more settled with what we are doing.

I look at my watch – fuck! I still have not set the correct time. What are we, two hours ahead of Greenwich Mean Time here?

"You OK back there, Hugo?"

"Of course I am not fucking OK back here!"

"Yes, all good." I keep my voice calm and confident.

Why is Femi's bag so much lighter than mine? I need to balance the weight a bit better otherwise I may put my neck out again. I also remember what I forgot to pack – sunglasses. Those alongside my common sense to turn and run as fast as I can back to London.

"I think we can find somewhere to rest over there in those disused buildings." Femi stands tall on a small sand mount and arches his back slightly to stretch it. He is pointing over to a few buildings in the far distance. At that moment, I hear a beeping sound coming from his pocket. He pulls out a mobile phone.

"I thought you said it was best not to bring a phone with me on the trip due to the nature of it. How come you get to bring one?" I catch up to where he is standing and I notice how much of a dwarf I must seem next to him as he is on the sand mount and I am standing below it. I see him quickly swipe open the phone, read some sort of text message, then close it quickly and return it to his trouser pocket.

"That's right, Hugo. No phone for you, but I need one exactly for moments like this."

I want to ask him if I can borrow his phone to call someone back home. To check in on a loved one. To perhaps call the dog minder to check on the dog. To call the office to tell them I will not be at the meeting. To let the guys know I can't make it to the drinks this evening. But all of those scenarios are in a make-believe world for me at present.

Femi turns to face me and looks down from his lookout post. The sun is high over his head and, from a distance it would perhaps look like I am worshipping some statue with this position.

"I have contacted my cousin. He owns a shipping transport business and will be able to get us safe passage to Cairo with him."

"What do you mean 'safe passage', Femi? What the hell is this turning into now?" I place the bags down next to me and slump down on my butt in-between them.

"I told you not to worry, this is all in hand. It's not how it was supposed to turn out, but it's all under control. I can trust my cousin and it will be safer going by river under his protection than making our way by road and other transport."

I know I must look pathetic sitting here like a kid having a hissy fit, but this is not what I signed up for. What was I taught to do in situations like this? Talk to my inner child, hold his hand, be kind and gentle with him and tell him it will be OK. Yeh, sure it will be OK. Fuck – will it?

"Come on, Hugo." I see the shadow of Femi's arm across my face as he reaches down to pull me up. "Let's get to those buildings and get a couple of hours' rest before we make our way down to the river."

"What's the time?"

"What's that on your wrist? Isn't your watch working?"

Femi flashes his fancy watch over to check the time.

"It's just gone 6.25."

So early in the morning and yet the sun is high and powerful already.

"Come on, Hugo." *"How many times have I heard him say that?"* "We can get a couple of hours' rest. I am sure the people the family were worried about will soon understand that it's not there anymore."

I am still not totally sure who is chasing us. But right now, I need to get out of the sun and rest. And more importantly, set my bloody watch to the right local time.

We draw close to the buildings that we spotted from a distance. The closer we get, it is clear that they do look very much abandoned. There is probably a collection of ten or so in total around this makeshift street. Most of the buildings are of single-storey build and have no or broken glass where the windows should be. I can see bars across most of the window cavities on closer inspection. Peeling paint of all manner of colours hangs from doorways and fences. Sand dunes have collected in the corners of the buildings and along some of the fence posts remaining.

One could be mistaken for thinking this is the film set of a great Western movie being prepped for shooting.

"Over here, Hugo." Femi walks to the side of one of the larger buildings and comes to stand in the shade, thankfully. "It all looks empty around here, but we can't be too sure. I will go and investigate and find where we can rest." He turns his back on me. "Help me take this off so you can guard it here."

I need to remember the instructions on this now, how to safely unbuckle and dismount the casing from his back and get it safely to the floor. I am sure this will not be the last time we will be doing this.

"I won't be long. Stay well out of sight here." I watch Femi disappear around the corner of the building while the casing, with the painting, lies here at my feet. Again, this is a perfect opportunity to get the hell out of here and make my way back to London. I have my passport and I am sure that I can trace back the way we came into the main town. I can leave the painting here for Femi to take care of. I will even leave him extra supplies of drinking water from my bag; that will help lighten my load in any case. I am sure he will understand. I mean, anyone with a rational mind would probably do the same thing in my situation, I am sure of it.

At least I am in the shade here. It is as cool as it could be, I suppose. My eyesight is now accustomed to the brightness of everything around me. I can see for miles, it seems. The sand dunes mix with the horizon of the sky in the distance. There is an eerie silence around here. It makes me feel very uncomfortable. I need the presence of others around to help drown out the thoughts and voices in me. The ones that echo and remind me of how the hurt and fear still rages within. I thought that out here it would be better for me and, up until now, it has not been as bad as the darkness in London, yet, now, right at this moment, I need something, I need some reassurance and belief that Femi is not like all the others and going to rip the trust away that I have placed in him. I came here on his reassurance and on his ability to make me trust him.

"What the fuck!" I jump at the tap on my shoulder from Femi behind me.

"Hugo, you OK? Didn't mean to frighten you. You seemed miles away."

I look at Femi and it takes me a second or two to remember where we are and who he is.

"Shit, man; don't sneak up on me like that." He does not look impressed and focuses on the painting on the floor.

"I have found somewhere to rest up for a bit. Come on; let's get out of the open. Help me get this back on."

It's a short walk across to a small building surrounded by a few smaller outbuildings. Again, there are missing windows around the sides of the building. The front door seems to be intact compared to many of the other structures. The door is wooden and has faded green paint peeling off it. The lower end of the door seems to have rotted away from the exposed atmospheric conditions. Various weeds and wild plantation sprout out from the ground and the cracks in the plasterwork of the building walls.

Femi leads the way through the door. My eyes take time adjusting to the darkness inside, contrasted with the reflecting sun bouncing off the outside walls. It is also so much cooler inside, which is such a relief.

"This is perfect for a few hours' rest." Femi walks into the open-plan room towards the far corner where a lonely chair rests.

At some stage in its life, the room must have been a place where someone would rest from the heat of the day. There is a small kitchen counter and sink at one end of the room with food and drink. There is a bed in the middle of the room, tucked up against the wall and one small wardrobe next to it. A worn-out rug lies at the foot of the bed with its Persian patterns still visible.

"Help me unbuckle this and get it onto this chair."

I do as I am told without questioning. I am too tired, dehydrated and sweaty to do anything else right now. Femi could ask me to stand on my head and I would probably try to do that without registering fully what he was asking.

"There is a small washroom through that door over there. You can have the bed to rest; I am more than happy and used to having the floor. I just need to confirm a few details with my cousin in relation to the meeting point along the river."

I am glad he let me have the bed, even though it is probably full of insects, I need some support for my back after all the walking. I see him pull out his mobile phone once again. For some reason, a rush of envy comes over me in seeing him do this. As I said, I am so used to being connected back in London. Perhaps that was part of the issue with my need to always check on what the outside world was doing and why they were not communicating with me. But here, without a phone, that burden has been lifted from me, but it doesn't change the fact that I can feel naked without it.

"The reception in here is poor. I am just going to step out to message him." He checks his watch and the phone for the time. "Let's say we aim to set off from here around

11.00 AM." With that he steps out and I slump onto the bed and sink into it as the mattress has lost any form of recoil properties.

I wake up with a sudden feeling of dread. My neck is wet with sweat and I look around. I don't remember how I drifted off so quickly. I can see Femi already up and looking through his bag.

He looks back over to me.

"That was good timing. Hope you slept. Go freshen up a bit. We need to get back on the move."

My head spins as I get up off the bed. My neck is stiff and I get a sudden chill down my neck and back as the sweat cools slightly now it's away from the mattress.

"Throw me a bottle of water, Femi." I take this into our luxury en suite bathroom...

"Hugo. You done in there?"

My thoughts are brought back to today with a knock at the door and the voice of Femi. He has such a thick accent from his home village.

"Be out in a few minutes," I answer.

"Well, get a move on." Femi's strong, confident voice again from the other side of the door. "We can't stay here any longer, it's not safe."

Standing up, I peel my shirt off. The sink is covered in dust and remnants of brickwork and plaster from the walls and ceiling. Struggling with the tap, as it is so stiff, I notice how weathered my fingers seem now. Managing to finally turn it, I feel the water on my face, which should have given me some relief. But it only reinforces the shit situation I find myself.

"Finally. You ready?" I walk out of the bathroom to find Femi checking the contents of his travel bags. He looks over to me when I don't answer.

"Look, Hugo, Don't worry. This is how it will be for a few more days, but we need to keep on the move…"

31

Now

Femi leaves me in a dimly lit room after we entered through the doorway. I did not get to see who opened the door as Femi's build was filling the whole entrance. There was no real dialogue either with whomever let us in; the door and gate were opened and Femi led the way through the narrow hallway into a room to the right. There was a small window looking out onto some sort of small courtyard encased with high walls all around and so there was not much natural light coming in. Femi told me to wait and he will be back in a few moments. He took the painting with him, still attached to his back with the casing.

Looking around, the room is small. It has the bare minimum of furniture. Two chairs that have worn fabric coverings and a small faded rug on the floor that I nearly trip over as the edges are rolled up. There are no pictures on the walls, just crumbling plaster and cracks. Over to the far wall is a wooden sideboard with a few ornaments on the surface. Brass horses and two jugs of various sizes. A solitary lonely light bulb hanging from a wire is in the centre of the ceiling.

Every inner aspect of me does not trust what is happening right now. I pat down my cargo trouser pocket and make sure my passport is still with me. Those words from Femi are bouncing around my skull, that he will protect me and look after me and for me to remember that. Running them over and over in my mind, forwards and backwards, to try to read between the lines and understand what he is trying to tell me, if anything. I know my true purpose of being here is yet to occur. I know I will soon be required to examine and appraise the painting. But what then? What then happens? Will I just be allowed to get onto a plane back to London, knowing that this painting has been stolen? Fuck! This is not a good situation I am in.

"Excuse me, sir."

I jump at the voice behind me from the doorway. A man of small stature holds a tray with a liquid-filled jug and ice cubes floating around, together with an empty glass.

"Some cool iced tea for you while you wait."

He moves past me, places the tray on the sideboard and pours the tea in the glass for me. He then turns and leaves the room without another word or look at me. It does look inviting to drink and it has reminded me of how dry my mouth is with my tongue sticking to the roof of it. It looks safe enough to drink. The glass has cooling condensation forming around the surface, calming to my fingers as I pick it up and savour the cool liquid on my lips.

I close my eyes while letting the liquid travel down my throat. Feeling every aspect of it lining the inside of me. It cools me slowly from within. My eyes give me the darkness and emptiness that I desire at the moment. How I would change every aspect of my circumstances right now to be alone, fearful, anxious, projecting, insecure, co-dependent and destructive back in London. Back where all those emotions cause me so much chaos – at least I know the comfort of those feelings in a familiar place. Here I have a new sensation that I have not felt before in myself. Here I feel the sensation of a resolution. I am fearful of what that resolution is though, as it is the unknown at present.

"Hugo." Femi's voice behind me awakens me from my futile daydream. I turn around and see him standing at the doorway, tall and confident, with no painting attached to his back. "Let's go, your time is here."

He leads the way, down the dark hallway towards the back of the building. We pass a couple of closed doors until we cross a kitchen and then out into an open courtyard. It is slightly bigger than the one I saw from the window of my room. The sun shines right down into this opening so the brightness hits my eyes and I need to squint as I follow Femi to the door that leads into a separate building. Femi holds the door open for me. As I go through, my eyes fix onto the structure that is in the centre of the room. Standing there alone with nothing surrounding it. It is highlighted with spotlights from above, but they do not focus on the object directly. The light gives just the perfect shine to the object without providing any direct glare.

The characteristic shape of a wooden easel stands in the middle of the room. The canvas is resting on the structure, now naked with no protective cloth covering, no protective casing. I look to Femi's face as he stands to the side of the door and then back to the canvas. My feet move slowly into the room. I feel the floor under my feet, but I cannot lift my feet fully off the floor and am aware that I am dragging them.

I feel Femi's hand on my shoulder and his voice.

"It is all yours, my friend, for as long as you need." I can tell from Femi's voice he is smiling as he says this. His footsteps leave the room followed by the sound of the door closing,

I take a sigh. I take a breath in. I fill my lungs and feel my heart beating away so forcefully as I come to terms with what I see with my eyes. I feel hesitant to go any closer, just in case my presence frightens it away. Just in case it disappears into small fragments of dust.

I can see the collection of materials resting on a table just to the far side of the easel. I recognise everything that I need to do the dating of the paint. Taking further steps closer, my hands are sweaty; not with the heat though, the temperature in this room is perfect. My hands are anxious. They are fearful of what they may handle soon.

The emotional blue rushes off the canvas to envelope the room. Just as Vincent wrote to his brother, Theo, at the time: *'The whole thing will be a symphony of blue and yellow.'*

The yellow of the sunflower heads in this painting look more subdued than the other *Sunflowers* paintings in the series. These here have much more of a sadness to them. But in the same essence they cry out that they are content, happy and free in that sadness. I can only imagine what Vincent tried to express in this piece. How he wanted so much to close the gap between what we feel and how we can express these feelings to each other. Looking at this now, I see how our inner sense of aloneness and frailties remind us to connect to each other.

As my eyes blink, I can't recall how I walked so close to the painting. I am standing a few centimetres from it now. My hand reaches to touch the surface, but I know I cannot with my skin, with the salt and humidity on my fingers. A pair of cotton gloves lay on the table to allow me to handle the masterpiece. The contents of my bag with paperwork and other aspects that I may need are also laid out on the table. My memory is blank as to when someone, most likely Femi, would have got my bag and done this. I must remember to breathe. I am conscious that I have been holding my breath for long periods of time now.

Oh Vincent, how you are so dearly missed. We really do not deserve to have the magic that you put into these art pieces to remind ourselves of what we hide within us and what we really run from. Standing here next to this *Sunflowers* painting, I feel reckless and stripped naked as a person, of everything I have been as a person. Why are all lessons in life taught to us in every minute of our existence, yet we only learn in the last moments of reflection?

I reach for the white gloves. My hands tremble as they pick the delicate garments up. No time for anxiety now. No time for self-doubt at this moment either. No room to be in the throws of apathy right now. There is no place for complacency on my part while I am in the presence of this masterpiece. In the presence of his own hand strokes, his fingers, his spirit that was poured into this.

I know the corner that I need to use for the blue paint extraction.

32

Now

The door opens slowly and a flood of sunlight rushes into the room. I see a large shadow of a figure standing at the doorway. It is the unmistakable silhouette of Femi. I am sitting on the floor, knees bent into my chest like a child who has just been told off. I look up at Femi as he slowly walks towards me. I cannot see his facial expression but I can imagine what it will be saying in its look, at present.

"Hugo."

I do not answer; I just stare at him as he walks closer and closer.

"You OK, Hugo?"

Still I do not answer.

He crouches beside me. I feel his hand on my arm. The pressure of it as comfort and safety. The heat from his hand radiates onto my arm and courses through my body. It sends a shiver down my spine to my buttocks that are in contact with the stone floor.

"Is it done?"

I can now see his expression. It is that of concern and uncertainty. His pupils are dilated in the darkness down here beside me.

The only word that I can formulate is,

"Yes."

Femi looks up over to the table just beyond the painting and then looks back to me. He gets up and walks over there. I left the three control jars and the two sample jars all lined up next to each other, alongside my notes of interpretation and detailed explanation of the results that occurred in each jar.

"Can I move the jars?" The question from Femi causes me slight confusion and my thoughts leak out into my words back at him.

"Why?"

There was a pause from Femi followed by a confused answer.

"I don't know. Suppose I just wanted to have a closer look at what change was occurring in the jars."

I can hear the shuffle of papers. He must be picking up my reports and reading through them.

"We need to go present your results now. Come on. You can educate us all."

He stands back over me, my reports in one hand and holding the other hand out to pull me up.

33

Now

I am placed back into the small, dark room with the lonely pathetic rug and chairs that are the only residents of the room.

"Let me take these to the curator to read." Femi holds on to the reports and leaves the room. I do not get the opportunity to ask anything or explain any aspect of my reports, but I think they are self-explanatory to anyone reading them.

The jug with iced tea has disappeared from the sideboard and there seems to be no sign of anyone coming to offer me anything now. Is this how it will be now? *My work is done.* No need to keep me in an especially safe state anymore.

I look out of the small, square window into the dull courtyard outside. In the distance I can hear the hustle of the bazaar that is just a stone's throw away, over these walls. I can hear faint sounds of talking and laughter from outside, but unable to make out what is being said. Unlikely that it is in English, in any case. There are strange sensations of emptiness and of aloneness rushing over me suddenly. Greater than any I have felt before. Only this time, I feel empty because I have no one to share the expression of my life's passion coming to a final reality and endpoint today. I have no one to share the reasoning that I was right for all this time. My thirst for the search and the truth was justified. This horrible, hollow feeling that I have succumbed to reinforces the fact that I have truly always been alone and have never settled those demons in me. Now the chase is finally over, I am left with those hollow beasts once again inside me, to eat away at me. Slowly and painfully, so that I feel every last cut and bite.

"Hugo. Please meet the curator."

I turn to see Femi standing at the doorway of the room with a man that I recognise, wearing a long, grey tailcoat with a white flower tucked into his lapel.

34

Now

My bag sits on the back seat of the car. Femi driving. I look out of the open passenger seat window. Watching the busy streets of Cairo pass me by. The people are still so busy around here. There seems no end to the activities and duties of everyone in this area. I feel like I am in a constant daydream at present, unable to put a coherent timeline together. The ride is bumpy and my stomach is empty.

The memories of London seem like a different lifetime now. I am unable to unravel the confusion of what has occurred and in what order and in what location. My head feels in a daze from the heat, from the confusion, from the dehydration, from it all.

I look down at my hands and notice that I have been rubbing my fingers together and the skin is raw around my nail bed now.

"What did he mean back there?"

I don't face Femi when I speak. He has been silent ever since we got in the car. A car waiting just outside the busy bazaar that we walked through. I think I am so over asking all the intimate details of this now.

"Which bit, Hugo? He said a few things back there."

"He is the same fucking guy that I saw in the

museum back in London. He speaks with a thick German accent. Is this the 'German' you mentioned who was after us?"

Femi takes a sharp left with the steering wheel and a car coming straight in our direction lets out a piercing horn of attention as we cut in front of its path. Femi seems unfazed by this.

"There were no Germans after us, Hugo."

I do not ask why he made me believe there was.

"The family. Where you stole the painting from. Is it the same family from Japan, during World War Two? They were defecting to America at the time."

I look over to Femi as he concentrates on the road. He does not respond to my words. He either doesn't know these details or is fully aware of everything. I continue.

"They defected before the bombing of Japan and they took all their valuable belongings with them. It was a very wealthy family. A family that had acquired a lot of expensive artefacts. Artefacts that, at the time, the Nazi force wanted to acquire for themselves at any cost."

I hope my words are burning into Femi right now. I look out the window, to our surroundings, and see we are leaving the city's safety now. Ahead lies open roads of sand-filled terrain and clear sky.

"You know the Nazi party came from Germany, right? Is it not a coincidence that the old guy back there is German and got you to steal this painting from that same family that defected at the time of the war?"

Still nothing from Femi.

"Tell me, Femi. He remarked back there that my work was done now. That the results and my conclusions were correct and that the painting was indeed the *Sunflowers* presumed destroyed in the bombing. But he asked you to complete the task now. What more is there left to do?"

Femi's jaw tightens and I am sure I can see him grip the steering wheel a bit tighter. The muscles in his forearms ripple with the tension; his tight skin enhancing the motions.

"I have a daughter. She went missing, Hugo. This was my way to find her, to get her back."

I know it is futile to ask anything more from Femi. He will not give anything else up.

35

Now

The feeling always comes to find you. It never leaves you. Always buried deep within, no matter how the time passes or how much work is done to try and get the demons to come out. It always comes to find you. Haunting the shadows in the mind. My whole life waiting for the answers to show me the light. Waiting for it all to make sense and then, as if by magic, everything is fixed. All those years, each day with that willingness to be found. But all I ever was and will remain is lost and never to be found. Buried underground, deep with all the dirt and fears that manifest in the unconscious.

I always knew that the last moments of my time on this earth would be the most important moments of self-reflection. When the intersections of life suddenly feel they have purpose. But, alas, even in these last few moments, these pathetic, pitiful handful of sand grains trickle through the fingers to indicate how delicate time is. Even now, at the end of it all, I still search for hope, for meaning, for some answers to help settle the unrest that lies within me.

How did I function for so long in such a state? The struggle of just being human. Now, in this position, I wonder why I didn't just end it all a long time ago. Each day felt so suffocating, but there was always this voice in my ear sitting on my shoulder telling me to hold on, it's not the end. Each time I would listen to it, I would convince my inner self that I would wake up thinking differently. But, each morning, for those tormented years, I was wrong. What did I hold on for? More importantly, what was I trying to search for, ultimately?

In these futile moments, I ponder on what I missed. What *did* I miss? Not in life, no, but what did I miss in myself? Why was I unable to unlock what I so desperately tried to discover within me? No matter how many hours I spent with Fiona in those therapy sessions, no matter how many glasses of gin Charlie and I had together, no matter how much I tried to convince myself I did not have a broken heart over her, whose name I still cannot whisper, and no matter how many times I would tell myself that there is always tomorrow, there is always the next day to make the change. To really become that new version of me. Somehow, I would find a way to make it through those dark nights , be that through alcohol, be that through nightmares or be that through running until I passed out in the cover of the night, I would find a way to make it through the frightful night. But now, I feel so exhausted from all those years spent chasing the answers to fix me from the outside world, from other aspects of validation. It has all led me here. Not being able to focus on tomorrow because there will not be a tomorrow. There is a strange ironic sensation of a slight freedom settling in, perhaps. In the knowledge that I will not need to face the struggle anymore. I will not need to feel the suffocation tightening in around me. The freedom perhaps of knowing that no longer do I have to pretend to suffer. No longer do I need to allow my fears to frighten me. For all that they caused. For all that they made disappear in my life. Now perhaps the freedom for me is in the forgiveness in them all.

Forgiveness for what was taken from me. Forgiveness for having my silence imposed on my life. Forgiveness for what might have been. Forgiveness for all we gave. Forgiveness for all the unforgettable acts of misunderstanding. I forgive them all for what was unleashed on me. I now see what Fiona meant with allowing forgiveness. The word, meaning and sentiment in that collection of letters allow my soul to be free. I forgive the torment that was imposed on me. I forgive the way my life was snatched away from me before I even knew what life was.

But, it still does not change the shallow feeling of everything that I could not let myself see. I did not allow myself to be seen and loved. I never made a sound and so I was never found by others. I was never found by myself. How could I ever expect others to find the better version of me if I did not dare do that for myself from the outset? Did I really prefer to be alone? Is that why I really did not want anyone to wait for me? Apart from her whose name I still refuse to mention to myself, even now at the end of it all. She came close. Well, at least I thought she was close enough. But was that also part of the master plan? Was I really just intending to cause that chaos around me? If I could not allow the real me out and deal with the real me, I would destroy all and anyone around me who saw the real me. Do I have time to focus on her in these last few seconds? Is she the one I voice my last few seconds for or do I have time to look at every aspect of interaction resulting in this outcome? Suddenly, all the literature I have ever read on my traumas, my projections, my wiring, is flooding back to me. Suddenly, all my neurones allow some gateways to open to unleash routes back to the past. Back to the hidden depths of my memory. Back to the core language that I should have developed to allow the real me to develop. To allow my true character to blossom. It was Fiona's favourite analogy, 'the butterfly coming out, slowly, ever so slowly from the chrysalis'.

Maybe now the core language will let me put things at peace. The feeling that this is the end, the feeling that I will be fine now and free, finally; maybe this is the moment that my core language comes so freely. Maybe this core language will let me put all those years into context. Yes, I feel a nice warm feeling of being golden from within me with this notion. It is so far from the other end of the spectrum that I travelled every day until now. Always on the ropes each day. Fighting for survival just to function. In the hope to attain peace from my own mind. To get some respite.

Forgiveness and saying thank you to all the traumas and the hurt that individuals inflicted on me is the way for me to set free. I did inflict pain on people on the way, for that I am truly sorry and for that I will forever be remorseful. But, I now see that that monster in me was not of my own making. It was inflicted on me. Will I have time now to allow all those people to pass through my thoughts, in peace, in freedom, in a manner that eases the pain for all? All the minefields that I walked through that kept me from the real me. All the minefields that I risked just to have normality. It became such a constant battle, I lost the essence of what I was searching for in the first place.

At least now, there is comfort in knowing that there are people with whom my trust aspects were confirmed.

That gives me peace, that gives me validation. I know if I could see myself right now, from up above, I would be smiling in the feeling that deep down 'I was OK'. Deep down, I surrounded myself with self-validation from others and that narrative was ultimately proven correct. The impending fear of abandonment that plagued my life. The unspeakable collection of emotions and feelings and fear that it evokes within. It is something that I will never be able to put into words. Regardless of having the core language to help aid me. Yes, my dependency on an alternative language, for my traumas, was rejection, projection and insecurity. The act of fear freezes you. I see that now. It freezes you in that moment. In that childlike state. Those seconds, minutes, hours of childlike static state when having that terror unleashed on me. In those moments, any form of coherent language was lost. Any hope of creating the appropriate, verbal response, was lost forever and locked without a way out. That inner child of me, that wounded inner child, that sweet innocent child that was supposed to be loved and nurtured into a safe place. That child only had visual acts of trauma to depend on. Visual acts of terror to learn from. Physical scars and pains to feel and to continue to feel forever, as it became that child's normality. Emotional regression that kept that child in that state. So now I see, if I was taken back to those nights of terror, to those nights when the ghost of me, as I child, stayed awake, standing in the stairway, in the dark, eyes filled with tears, listening to the screams from downstairs, not understanding, not knowing how to voice anything, I see that that child was addicted to that pain. Those tears were not because of the fear. Those tears were not because of the terror. Those tears became tears of addiction. Of needing to experience the pain. To feel the guilt, the dirt, the shame and feel I needed to be used. That was what became of that child. That is what that child, in me, saw as validation. And that is what I unleashed on all those that came close to me during my adult life. Now, in these last moments, I see the true core language that I should have had as a child. The words that I so desperately needed to shout. The words that only now I see I can learn.

I never could remember many of my dreams; it feels that this perhaps is a dream that I am having or rather a nightmare that seems to have an end. A finality to it, for once. I always wondered what my last thoughts on earth would be. What the last dream passing through my conscious mind would be. I was always chasing the future but not wanting to settle my past. I was perhaps always wanting this day to come too soon, too prematurely, as all I ever did was think of the next moment. Now it feels it is here, do I try and hold on to it for as long as I can? Savour the moment. Live in the present for once in my lifetime. The pain and fear and suffocating is starting to settle as the realisation dawns that this may mean the end is near.

I can feel my unconscious mind being free now, letting the doors open and all the memories run wild to my consciousness. At last, Fiona was right; my mind is free and ready to tackle all the previous darkness. I feel so light; the air around me feels so effortless. I can feel the wind rush past me. It whistles as it gushes past my ears. It has a calming nature to it. It evokes the sensation in my soul that I am rushing to my destination and making lots of great time and distance to get there. My hair moves and tugs with the change of direction in this wind. It reminds me of when she would pull at my hair when we would be in bed together. In the middle of making love, her fingers would run through my hair, she would gently at first take a few strands between her fingers and twist them around. Then she would reach down to the lower aspect of my head and pull hard on the ends of my hair. I would look into her eyes as she did this. Her eyes in the moonlight sky as it flooded through the bedroom window. The moonlight would invade our space in those moments and create a blanket of passion for us both to be wrapped in. I feel the same sensation now as the small hairs on my arms stand up and I feel goose bumps running along the length of them. How I would feel this electricity while she would lock her legs around me, around my waist, tight, not allowing me to escape. She would draw me in with her force. Her back would arch and our eyes would be locked. Locked in that moment that seemed like forever. Seemed to be perfect. Seemed to be safe. So vulnerable in that moment yet feeling so content and at peace. Our sweaty bodies became one in that moment. She would whisper in my ear as she pulled my head close to her. She would whisper those words that I have always longed to be, to have, to hear. Her eyes would soften and dilate in the moonshine and her lips would move in slow motion as she spoke the words, *"Let's make a baby."* That same calmness of safety comes over me now, in my last moments as I want to reach out and hold her hands once again, fingers tightly interlaced within each other and I want to say the words that I could never say back then. I want to say that I will be a better me. I want to say I will be a new version of me. I want to say I do want to be loved. I want to say that I do want her to love me. I want to say that I will learn to love her how I know I can.

I feel a sudden rush of vertigo and nausea and bile reaches my throat. Lasts all but a second; now I am back to the calmness of thought. How I learnt the aspect of being present in the moment and remaining calm from my new friend, Femi. This most unlikely circumstances of friendship forged out of a situation that was so unpredictable. The kindness and empathy that he created around me allowed me to understand what trust is. Allowed me to breathe with the notation of how trust between two people can develop and be tested simultaneously. How to allow our inner battles to make us regain the fullness of that trust. I feel a smile form across my face as I think back to how much I pushed that trust boundary. Always guessing and second-guessing his intentions. How he protected me repeatedly so that I would stay safe, so that I would stay calm. He read me. He could read my emotions and the impulses that were secondary to such impulsive decisions and words from me. He showed me and taught me patience, endurance and resilience. True friends give time and space when it is needed and do not falter from that line. They guard the path to bringing you back on the right track. How Femi did this time and time with me. In that short time of our friendship, how he held my hand and allowed me to walk or run when it suited, yet always made sure I did not trip. How I learnt his expressions, mannerisms, emotions and moods and how it reflected in his behaviour to the outside world. How I wanted to also be there for him at times of struggle. How I also wanted to feel proud to guide him, as my friend, to a better place. He taught me this. Femi – my friend – he made me understand what a true, trusting dynamic friendship is.

I feel my eyes rush with tears and am unable to keep

them fully open at present. The burning force of the wind that surrounds me, hits the cornea of my eyes. Forcing me to close my eyes again. The darkness enhances the sound howling around me. It seems to be getting stronger and stronger. Louder and louder. Closer and closer. So close I feel like reaching out with my hands and catching it in my palms to feel the strength of the sound in my hands. My arms feel pinned to my side. All my power is used to try to pull my arms out in front of me, but the force of something is just too powerful to allow them to be free. I can do this. I will try again, just to feel the power of this force all around me. It feels so powerful and frightening due to the force, but it makes me feel so liberated and so free at last…

36

Before

"Femi… I," I am trembling. My words hardly come out. We have stopped in the middle of nowhere. The desert surrounds us in all directions. The sand dust that lies in the wake of the tyres kicks up around us. I can't look at him at all. My mouth is so dry now that I fear it will get stuck shut together if I do not have water soon. I look down at my hands resting on my lap and notice that I have been pressing them against each other so hard that there is a torn bit of skin.

I remember I was saying something to Femi.

"Femi, I do not understand. Wh…what are we doing here?" I can't stop this trembling feeling I have inside. I feel like my heart is going to jump out of my chest. It is causing such pain, a crushing pain in my chest. I want to hold it with my hand to make it stop. I now know the pain that she experienced when I broke her heart. I saw her clutch her chest and sit on the floor when she thought I had broken all trust with her. I never quite understood that motion of hers until right now. How when something frightens you so much that you literally feel your heart breaking. I feel that same sensation now, sitting here in this car, in the middle of nowhere with a man whom I trusted as a friend all this time. I can feel the impending doom enveloping me. I know exactly what we are doing here, but I desperately want Femi to create doubt in that for me. I want him to tell me an alternative ending to this story.

He switches off the engine. Still not saying a word and still not facing me. He just sits there. Hands resting on the steering wheel, looking out to the horizon ahead. The sky is clear blue with not even a whisker of a cloud to be seen. The sun is high in the sky, shining down all around and creating this beautiful environment. Picture-postcard, but the terrain is harsh and demanding to tolerate in reality. I notice that we have parked on what seems to be the verge of a deep cliff edge, as the land ahead of us is at such a lower level than us.

Looking back over to Femi, I see his eyes are closed tight. His arms are still resting on the steering wheel and it seems he is in prayer. He has sweat pouring off his face. His arms strong and tense while he sits there. He tenses his jaw; I see his facial muscles contract and then he opens his mouth. But, still he does not speak.

"Femi, please; what the fuck is all this?"

My voice is higher-pitched than I intended. I look over to the back of the car through the rear window to see if I had missed anything. To look for any clue of what this is. To see if there is any other car coming for a meeting we had arranged. But it is all in a futile effort as, deep down, I know what this is. Out of nowhere, a flock of birds get my attention. They fly in from my right, go high over the car and then swoop down at great speed and precision to disappear over the cliff edge. I wait, watching for them to reappear, but they do not.

"Please. Get out of the car. We need to walk a bit."

I am sure I just heard Femi's voice. It caught me unaware.

"What was that?" I prompt him to speak again.

He sighs. "Do not make this harder than it already is, Hugo. Out of the car, please."

I reach for where my seat belt should be, to stall the need to get out, but I see that I wasn't wearing the belt in the first place. I take another look at Femi, but still, no reaction from him. I push the door open slowly and another rush of heat hits me. I swing my legs around and step out of the car. My trusted boots, still going strong, crush the dry gravel and sand on the ground. I turn to look back into the car, placing my hand on the roof of it, but withdraw sharply due to the sheer heat of it. I wait now for the next instruction from Femi.

I wait, standing there, looking back into the car. I am sure I make out Femi clutching the steering wheel so hard with his hands. It makes his arms shake with the force of the grip he has on the wheel. He then suddenly flings the door open and steps out of the car. He looks much smaller of a man now than he ever has. His shoulders are rounded and compressed into himself as he stands across over on the other side of the car with his back to me. He eventually walks around to the front of the car and sits on the bonnet.

"You know, as a boy I always believed that the desert contained another world hidden under all the sand dunes." His voice is soft. "I would run into the sand and just dig and dig at the mountains of sand, convinced that I would uncover a secret doorway to take me deep below the surface and then eventually find a new civilisation."

I go and sit beside him on the bonnet of the car. The heat is not as much as I had expected from the car.

"Did you ever find it?"

"Find what?" Femi asks, still looking down at the floor ahead of him.

"The doorway you were looking for. In the sand."

He lets out a little chuckle, followed by a deep sigh.

"I always knew that it was all in my head. I knew in reality there would be no door, there would be no alternative world or civilisation. But..." He pauses. I can feel the heat from his arm as it rests next to my pathetic skinny one. I nudge him with my arm by leaning into him.

"Come on, finish what you were saying." I will him to carry on so I can think that there is an alternative narrative to all this. If I close my eyes, I can just picture us back sitting in a bar, in London, just as friends, after a day's work.

"But it gave me a different view on my life back then. As a kid. It took me away from the reality of what I faced everyday then. To think that there was a world without hunger, without the fear of being kidnapped every day, without the worry of war over and over again in my village."

This is the first time he has spoken of any childhood areas of his life. Of his struggles, also. Why is he doing this now? Does he feel it will give me comfort? Does he feel it will open up another door of trust between us? The thought just invades my mind. Did my unconscious sense the unrest in Femi's past? Is that why I felt I could trust him and to be his friend? Once again, did I attract the fractured person to give me that security?

Femi places his hands over his face. His fingers pressing his eyes. I dare not look directly at him just in case I get a glimpse of his weakness at this moment. I want to remember that he is strong in character and that I could be carried by his determination and strength.

He lets out a sigh.

"Hugo." His voice is tired. It's heavy. It seems lost like it has travelled all these miles out here in the heat, in the dust and the sand of the desert and it's finally had enough. The sound of my name from his lips now makes me unsettled within myself.

He continues, "There is a river, flowing down there, over that edge." Still he does not face me. I know why he is telling me. I know the reason of this conversation. I will inside, even now, defend him as my friend. To take him out of this inevitable decision.

"Maybe you were looking in the wrong places." My sentence confuses Femi.

"What? What do you mean, Hugo?"

"Maybe the secret door and the civilisations were not buried in the sand dunes at all, but deep underwater in the rivers. A magical, mystical world deep underwater."

The words sit there between us. The time and space between us allows us to indulge in the guilty pleasure of wishing for a better alternative world.

I get up off the car bonnet and slowly walk to the edge of this plateau. I reach a few feet from the edge and catch a glimmer of the river, winding its course deep below us. There are specks of green lush trees and bushes scattered along its course. I kick a mound of dust and stones over the edge. I hear the car door close behind me. I resist turning around to see my friend for one last moment.

"Hugo!" Femi shouts from the car. "Let me know how perfect the world is under the water."

The sound of the car fades behind me. I can hear it

disappear into the distance, but I do not turn around. I close my eyes. I feel the heat all around me. I become more aware of the sound of emptiness that surrounds me. There is a sense of contentment of the stillness of this wilderness. I want to hold on to this feeling.

I do not know what drove my legs to move, but I notice I am walking forward, taking small steps in front of me. My eyes still closed. Still having that sense of safety within me. I do not even think of the edge. I picture the beautiful pure water of the river that flows below. I do not even notice that this step has no ground for me to land on.

37

Now

My face feels the force. For the first few seconds it feels like a basketball being thrown directly at me by Hercules. I feel the burning of the impact spreading all over my chest, arms, abdomen and legs. Then as quickly as the impact was felt, it disappears and a sensation of calmness once again envelops me. A continuous muffled effect has replaced the howling sound. I cannot place this sound. This sound seems to also cover me like a blanket. Holding me tight, wrapped in its grip with no way of escaping it, no matter which way I try to manoeuvre. There is something unnatural about how my environment is now. My body movements seem to be so laboured and slow in nature. I can picture how I want to move, yet when trying to put it in practice, it is like my body feels disconnected from my brain and the signals willing the commands.

My chest feels tightness, a pressure being drilled in from all directions. Taking a deep breath is no use to ease this sensation. Opening my mouth, I feel as though this new sound rushed in through my open mouth and infiltrates down my throat and into the far dark recesses of my lungs. Now I can picture the pressure pushing from the inside of my lungs as well as the pressure pushing in from outside, down onto my chest. I want to be taken back to the free feeling of a few moments ago. This replacement sensation is very unsettling for me.

Could these be my last moments? This suffocating emotion again. What was it Fiona taught me to try to picture when I get like this? To think of how I would care for my inner wounded child. To show the little Hugo in me, the child Hugo whom just wanted to be a child all those years ago. How I should be gentle with myself. I picture that Hugo. I picture that child now. How I would comfort that child to say that it was never his fault. How I would let that child feel loved, feel cared for, feel free to laugh, free to explore the wonders of life. How I would want that child not to feel the panic of being made to be an object. How I would remove the manipulation and conditioning placed upon that young Hugo. How I would surround that child with the language of emotion that needs to be developed with the appropriate exposure of learning and teaching. How I would replace the fear and pain and torment and abandonment that child was exposed to with laughter, with happiness, with hugs and with the simple feeling of safety.

The technique worked. I suddenly feel that freedom and peace coming over me again. The pressure feeling has settled. I no longer feel the pain and fear of the child version of me. No longer do I feel the betrayal of trust by my friend, Femi. I no longer punish myself for her lack of patience and understanding with me, the real broken me and how she abandoned me when I showed all of me.

The pressure feels so calm to me. No longer do I need to gasp for air. No longer do I have to take deep breaths.

Sleep calls me. Sleep at last calls me. This is the sensation I have longed for all these years. Contentment.

It calls me with open arms now. It wants to comfort me now forever and no longer will I battle with it. No longer will I fear the night, the darkness or emptiness and stillness. I welcome it with an open heart now. I feel so empowered to succumb to the calling of it. One last glance at the world around me. I open my eyes. I see the beautiful blue calmness of water all around me. I see the light shining through the layers of clear crystal water towards me. My blinking becomes more and more laboured and lazy. A nice laziness like laying in a grass field watching the sunset on a summer's evening.

My vision goes black with a blink of my eyes. I see the child I once was, happy, laughing so hard that my face turns red and my stomach aches. I see that child running with a kite through the fields with the wind making my hair float behind me.

I open my eyes for a second, the calmness of the water still surrounds me and I smile. I close them again. The vision I now see is my friend smiling and laughing with me as we discuss the merits of working to live versus living to work. My friend, Femi, holds a drink in his hand and I smile at this man who has taught me so much in such little time.

My eyes now more difficult to open. So I close them again. This vision is of her. Her smile radiates all across the room as she spots me walking into the coffee shop to meet her. The tight embrace as she runs to greet me. The feel of her hair on my face. The smell of her. That distinctive smell that lingers on me for days. The vision of me looking into her eyes. Those eyes, endless.

I feel at ease, finally. I feel I can finally sleep. My last thought as I drift into this forever sleep. My letter to Vincent:

Dear Mr Vincent van Gogh,

I am Hugo Jensen, aged ten years old. I wish you could read my letter. Your paintings are so beautiful. I look at them in all the books we have at school. I try to touch the pages to feel the brush strokes. I know it is silly because there is no way that I could actually feel the painting in those books. I read so much about your paintings and your life and I am sad that I cannot be your real friend as I feel you would understand me. I think how I could sit and watch you paint for hours and when your paint runs out, I could run and mix you more colours so that you can carry on painting. In the evenings, after you have finished painting, we could go for long walks in the fields and think of more things to paint for the next day.

I have decided I will try to paint your The Starry Night *painting for school. I look at that painting for hours. I have a small cutting of it that I keep in my pencil case and every time I need to feel happy, I pull it out and look at it. At night, I look out of my window and try to make the sky change to look like your painting. It never works, but it makes me smile because I keep seeing your painting when I close my eyes in bed.*

I will draw the painting and I will look after it forever and ever and ever. I will make sure I look at it every night so that it will stay in my mind and help me sleep.
Your best friend,
Hugo Jensen.

****

Vincent van Gogh whispered to his brother, Theo, as he died in his arms on July 29th 1890 at 1.00 AM...

"The sorrow will last forever."

Vincent van Gogh born March 30th 1853, died July 29th 1890, aged 37 years.

Aleksandr lives in London, UK. Having a passion and fascination of history and how that is reflected in culture around the world, he focuses his writing on that view point.

His career has spanned many backgrounds that he encompasses in his writing. Having being involved in the medical world, creative industries of film and music and also balancing his real passion of humanitarian work, he finds all those aspects as inspiration for his writing.

Focusing now on bringing all that his inner passion and reflection has taught him to share in his writing with others. He is embarking on writing a series of novels with a narrative of meaning and thought.

He is a keen health advocate and exercise enthusiast with an addiction to all things that taste like coffee!

"Writing gave me the door to help unravel the aspects that our brain cortex locks away, deep within us, to alter how we interact with others and the world around us. Fearful events, trauma and hurt that we do not process correctly can cause pain for those around us that care. It is very easy to project pain in others and our surroundings if we do not look within us first. It has now become a lifelong mission for me to become a better version of me and continue to value important lessons to always be learnt. Human interaction needs to always make us reflect and better ourselves."

Please scan the QR code below
to take you to more books by Aleksandr
and to leave any comments or reviews

Also available from Alexsandr Jarid

FATEFUL
HOPE

LIFE. TO BE BORN AND GIFTED THE ABILITY TO FEEL HUMAN. TO LOVE, CRY AND CREATE NEW LIFE. THIS IS HUMANITY. OR IS IT ALL JUST A LIE?

Cameron and Emilie. Two individuals who seem to meet by chance. A path that started out so perfect, spirals into a web of deception, kidnap and death. Emilie disappears and the time that follows, takes Cameron into the dark world of powerful forces that leverage on Emilie to get Cameron to reveal secrets he hid that they deem their property. Associates and friends who Cameron held close to his heart, all come into the frame and not all ever was what it seemed. Now he must consider, who or what to believe if he is to get Emilie back safely and all that Emilie now holds for his own future family. This is not just about two people fighting for love and survival. They both realise that this is about the survival of humanity and all that it holds in its past for our future.

Coming soon from Alexsandr Jarid

NEW HOPE

Intelligent, independent, focused and with a passion for life. Siena has everything going for her. Surrounded by friends who are her only family and together they are working on ground breaking research that could change the face of humanity. What is there not to love about her life?

But, all is not settled under her surface. The darkness that has cursed her parents now hunts her. The shadows rise and Siena now faces the greatest test of her life. Pushing her mental, emotional and physical attributes to her breaking point. A guardian from the past arrives to protect her against an evil that is not what it seems. Siena soon realises there is no present state, only that of the past and what lays ahead in the future.

Coming soon from Alexsandr Jarid

23 MINUTES

Have you ever wondered why you make certain choices in life and not others?

How certain are you that the choices you make are indeed made by you and not some other force outside your conscious control?

What may seem like an unimportant event at a moment in your day, may actually have profound consequences from there onwards which you will not understand for many years yet.

It took 92 years for him to find the true meaning of 23 minutes of his life that altered his world. A world that involved the globe, power, death but ultimately 23 minutes of pure love and lemons.